A Word from Stephanie
About Breaking the Rules

Having a date is *great*, right? And having a date with the most popular, coolest, cutest boy in the whole ninth grade is the *absolute greatest*. Right again? Well, now I'm not so sure. Kyle Sullivan has finally asked me out. I am the envy of every girl in school. The only trouble is, Kyle has some really strange ideas. Like, he thinks boys get to make the rules about dates—and decide everything *their* way. Hmmm. Maybe Kyle hasn't heard that some rules are made to be broken.

Guess I'll have to break the news to Kyle. In the meantime, let me tell you about something that *isn't* any trouble. My family. My very big family.

Right now there are nine people and a dog living in our house—and for all I know, someone new could move in at any time. There's me, my big sister, D.J., my little sister, Michelle, and my dad, Danny. But that's just the beginning.

When my mom died, Dad needed help. So he asked his old college buddy, Joey Gladstone, and my uncle Jesse to come live with us to help take care of me and my sisters.

Back then, Uncle Jesse didn't know much about taking care of three little girls. He was more into

rock 'n' roll. Joey didn't know anything about kids, either—but it sure was funny watching him learn!

Having Uncle Jesse and Joey around was like having three dads instead of one! But then something even better happened—Uncle Jesse fell in love. He married Rebecca Donaldson, Dad's co-host on his TV show, *Wake Up, San Francisco*. Aunt Becky's so nice—she's more like a big sister than an aunt.

Next Uncle Jesse and Aunt Becky had twin baby boys. Their names are Nicky and Alex, and they are adorable!

I love being part of a big family. Still, things can get pretty crazy when you live in such a full house!

FULL HOUSE™: Stephanie novels

Phone Call from a Flamingo
The Boy-Oh-Boy Next Door
Twin Troubles
Hip Hop Till You Drop
Here Comes the Brand-New Me
The Secret's Out
Daddy's Not-So-Little Girl
P.S. Friends Forever
Getting Even with the Flamingoes
The Dude of My Dreams
Back-to-School Cool
Picture Me Famous
Two-for-One Christmas Fun
The Big Fix-up Mix-up
Ten Ways to Wreck a Date

Available from MINSTREL Books

FULL HOUSE™ Stephanie

Ten Ways to Wreck a Date

Peter Landesman

A Parachute Press Book

A MINSTREL® BOOK

Published by POCKET BOOKS
New York   London   Toronto   Sydney   Tokyo   Singapore

This book is a work of fiction. Names, characters, places and incidents are products of the author's imagination or are used fictitiously. Any resemblance to actual events or locales or persons, living or dead, is entirely coincidental.

A MINSTREL PAPERBACK *Original*

A Minstrel Book published by
POCKET BOOKS, a division of Simon & Schuster Inc.
1230 Avenue of the Americas, New York, NY 10020

A PARACHUTE PRESS BOOK

READING Copyright © and ™ 1996 by Warner Bros.

FULL HOUSE, characters, names and all related indicia are trademarks of Warner Bros. Television © 1996.

ISBN: 0-671-53548-X

First Minstrel Books printing April 1996

10 9 8 7 6 5 4 3 2 1

A MINSTREL BOOK and colophon are registered trademarks of Simon & Schuster Inc.

Cover photo by Schultz Photography

Printed in the U.S.A.

CHAPTER
1

◆ ◢ ◢ ◆

"Ahh, my favorite period of the day." Stephanie Tanner sighed happily. She balanced an empty tray against her hip. "Lunchtime in the beautiful middle school cafeteria."

Stephanie was waiting in the lunch line with her two best friends, Allie Taylor and Darcy Powell.

"Did you just say this place was beautiful?" Allie asked. A stray piece of wavy brown hair fell in her eyes as she stared at the familiar room. Stephanie knew that Allie saw the same dull walls and long green tables as always.

"I don't think Steph means the cafeteria," Darcy said. She grinned, and her white teeth flashed against her dark skin. She nudged Stephanie from behind. "She thinks the *scenery* is beautiful."

"You're right." Stephanie sighed again. "Any place is beautiful when Kyle Sullivan is in it."

Kyle Sullivan was in the lunch line ahead of them. Stephanie couldn't stop staring at him. Kyle was a ninth grader. A gorgeous ninth grader. Stephanie had a huge crush on him. And today Stephanie thought he looked even cuter than usual. He was wearing a cool pair of cutoff denim shorts, bright green high-top sneakers, and a black T-shirt. His blond hair was long enough to curl against his neck.

"Well, Stephanie, are you ready to try asking Kyle on another date?" Darcy asked.

"I don't know." Stephanie shook her head. "Don't forget what happened last time. I don't think I could survive another disaster like that one."

A while ago Stephanie had actually worked up the courage to ask Kyle on a date. But she'd been so nervous, she'd completely messed up. Kyle had asked out someone else instead—the girl standing right next to Stephanie. It was one of the worst moments of her life.

"It won't be like last time," Darcy assured her.

"That's right," Allie agreed. "Kyle likes you

now. He smiles at you whenever he sees you. And he *did* send you that valentine."

"What did it say again?" Darcy asked, pretending not to remember. "Was it, *To a great partner*—"

"No," Stephanie said. "It was, *I couldn't have picked a better—or cuter—earth science partner.*" Stephanie smiled. She remembered how excited she'd been about the valentine. It had been read on the radio as part of a special Valentine's Day show.

"Oh, that's right." Darcy chuckled. "I remember now."

"You know Kyle likes you," Allie said. "So why not try to ask him out again?"

"Yeah, you should, Steph," Darcy said. "You almost did it before. If you ask him out now, he'll probably, definitely say yes."

Stephanie smiled at her two best friends. It was great to have them around to give her advice. Stephanie and Allie had been best friends for nine years. They had met on their first day of kindergarten. They had lots in common. They both loved music, reading, and funny movies. But most of all, Stephanie liked Allie's calm and sensible way of looking at things.

Darcy was totally different from Allie. Darcy had a wild sense of humor. She was lively and fun to be around. Sometimes she went a little overboard. But she was a loyal friend. Together Darcy, Allie, and Stephanie made an incredible team.

"I *could* ask Kyle out again," Stephanie told Allie and Darcy. "But why hasn't *he* asked *me* out yet?"

"He sent the valentine," Darcy pointed out. "Maybe the next move is yours."

"Maybe. Or maybe this isn't the right time to ask him out," Stephanie said.

"Maybe you're just making excuses," Darcy replied.

"Okay." Stephanie gave in. It was no use arguing with Darcy when she had her mind made up. "Why don't I ask him to go rollerblading Saturday night?"

"That would be great!" Darcy grinned.

Just then there was a commotion in the line ahead of them. Stephanie saw a flash of pink. A loud, high-pitched voice ordered some kids to step aside.

"Renee Salter! Can you believe her?" Darcy shook her head. "Renee thinks she can cut in line whenever and wherever she wants. Those Flamingoes think they run this school or something."

"They sort of do." Allie giggled.

The Flamingoes were a group of the coolest, most popular girls at John Muir Middle School.

They hung out together. And they always wore pink. Stephanie had actually been invited to join their club back in sixth grade.

But the Flamingoes were really pretty awful. They had asked Stephanie to steal her father's phone card so one of them could make long-distance calls to her boyfriend. When Stephanie realized what the Flamingoes were really like, she quit. Now she and the Flamingoes weren't on very good terms.

Stephanie strained her neck to see what Renee was up to this time.

"Oh, no!" Stephanie cried. "Renee's cut in line— right in front of Kyle!"

Stephanie knew that Renee liked Kyle. Everyone in school knew it. But Kyle hadn't asked her on a date. Of course, that didn't mean that he wouldn't ask—someday. Renee was also a ninth grader. And she was popular. And beautiful.

And pushy, Stephanie thought.

"That's it!" Stephanie exclaimed. "No way is this going to happen a second time. If Renee can cut in line, so can I."

"Way to go, Steph!" Allie cried.

"This is the nineties," Darcy added. "Go for your man!"

Stephanie stepped out of line and walked up to

Kyle and Renee. Luckily Kyle was standing right in front of Sue Kramer. Stephanie knew Sue pretty well. Last year they were the only seventh graders chosen to be on the *Scribe*, the middle school newspaper.

"Can I borrow this spot for a second?" Stephanie asked Sue.

"Sure," Sue replied. "If I didn't have to eat, I'd let you have it forever."

Sue made room and Stephanie slipped into line right behind Kyle. She was about three inches away from him. She took a deep breath.

Okay, it's now or never, Steph, she told herself. *You can do it!*

Stephanie reached out her hand.

I can't believe I'm about to touch Kyle Sullivan on the back! Stephanie thought, almost giggling. She cleared her throat. "Uh—" she began.

"Hey, Kyle," Renee suddenly said. "What are you doing this weekend?"

It had happened again!

Stephanie's mouth dropped open—but no sound came out. Quickly Stephanie clamped her mouth shut.

This is like a curse, she thought. *Every time I try to ask Kyle out, another girl gets there first!*

Stephanie slipped out of line. She headed

straight for the cafeteria doors. She was leaving, and fast. She would have to explain to Darcy and Allie later. No way could she spend a single moment more in the cafeteria. Not when Renee was busy planning a date with Kyle. A date that should have been Stephanie's!

CHAPTER
2

◆ ◂ ▪ ◆

As soon as Stephanie got home that afternoon, she went to the kitchen. She hadn't eaten a thing at lunch. By the end of the school day she'd been starving. Her stomach was grumbling so loudly one of her teachers snapped at her for talking in class!

Stephanie polished off a bowl of chocolate ripple ice cream. She grabbed her book bag and hurried upstairs. The bedroom door was shut. Stephanie knocked and turned the knob. Nothing happened. She turned the knob again. Still nothing.

What's going on?

"Hey!" Stephanie cried, pounding on the door.

Loud music came from inside the bedroom. Stephanie recognized it. It was from one of Michelle's sing-along records.

"Michelle?" she called. "Are you in there? Open up! You know the rule: *No . . . locked . . . doors!*"

Stephanie rattled the door handle and knocked even harder.

"Michelle," she said. "You'd better open this door or else!"

Stephanie had raised her hand to knock again when the door suddenly swung open. Her nine-year-old sister stood in front of her with a huge grin on her face.

"What are you smiling at?" Stephanie frowned. "You know you're not allowed to lock this door. This is partly *my* room, too!"

And it would be all *my room if I ever got my way,* Stephanie thought.

"*V-a-c-u-u-m,*" Michelle said.

"What?" Stephanie asked. She brushed past Michelle and dumped her books on her desk.

"*V-a-c-u-u-m.* That's the word I won the spelling bee with," Michelle announced proudly.

"Congratulations, Michelle," Stephanie replied, rolling her eyes. "I bet Dad was really proud of *that* one. Maybe he'll even *buy* you a vacuum for your next birthday." Their father, Danny Tanner, was a total neat freak. He was always dusting, scrubbing, washing, or vacuuming something.

"My teacher gave me a big silver star sticker," Michelle continued. "With glittery stuff all over it."

"Fine," Stephanie replied. "But you still aren't allowed to lock this door."

"It said, *Michelle Tanner—Spelling Champion*," Michelle finished.

"Okay, okay." Stephanie sighed. "That's really great, Michelle." She paused. "But you have to turn that music down. I have a ton of homework to do. And I can't hear myself think in here."

"I can't hear you think either," Michelle replied.

Stephanie groaned. "You're not supposed to, Michelle. It's just a figure of speech. It means I can't concentrate."

"Oh. Okay," Michelle said. She turned off the music.

But Stephanie still couldn't concentrate on her homework. She kept seeing visions of Kyle and Renee. Every time she glanced at a textbook she saw them instead—dancing under the stars or holding hands on a romantic ocean cruise.

Her imagination was *definitely* getting the best of her. She tapped her pencil against her desk. *Focus,* she told herself. The pencil slipped from her fingers and went flying backward over her shoulder.

Stephanie got up and crossed the room. She bent down to pick up her pencil. "Yuck! What's this?" she cried.

Under her bed was a big blob of half-eaten food.

"Oh, gross!" Stephanie picked the food off the floor. It looked as if it had once been a cupcake.

"Michelle!" Stephanie lifted the half-eaten thing with her fingertips. "This is disgusting!"

"Ooops!" Michelle's eyes popped open wide. "Dad gave me the cupcake when he saw my spelling bee star," Michelle said. "I shared it with Comet. But I guess he didn't like it."

Comet was the Tanner family's golden retriever. And there was a strict family rule about what Comet was allowed to eat.

"Michelle, you know you're not supposed to feed Comet junk food," Stephanie scolded. "And there's no eating in the bedroom, either!"

The phone across the hall started ringing. Stephanie dropped the cupcake into the trash can and ran into her older sister D.J.'s room.

"Ugh!" Stephanie grunted as she picked up the phone. There were cupcake crumbs stuck to her fingers. The crumbs were wet with Comet's drool.

"Steph? Is that you?" Allie's voice came over the line.

"Are you okay?" Darcy asked.

It was both of her friends, using Allie's three-way calling.

"I'm fine." Stephanie sighed. "Michelle's just driving me crazy, as usual. And breaking all the house rules. *First* she locked me out of my own room. And *then* I found a half-eaten cupcake under my bed."

"Gross," Allie said.

"Plus she gave the cupcake to Comet and it was covered with dog drool."

"Double gross," Darcy said.

"I shouldn't be surprised," Stephanie said. "Not after all the bad stuff that happened to me today."

"Speaking of today, why did you run out of the cafeteria?" Allie asked.

"And why didn't you wait to walk home with us?" Darcy added.

"Sorry I ducked out on you guys." Stephanie told them everything that had happened. "I just couldn't talk about what happened in the cafeteria. I don't even want to think about it."

"You do seem to have pretty bad luck when it comes to talking to Kyle," Darcy admitted.

"Yeah. I should probably stop hoping I'll *ever* go on a date with him," Stephanie said.

"Maybe he'll still ask you out," Allie suggested.

"It doesn't look like that's ever going to happen," Stephanie replied.

"Wait a minute," Darcy teased. "I thought you were just waiting for the right moment to ask him yourself."

"Sure," Stephanie said, kicking off her shoes and flopping down on D.J.'s bed. "Only the right moment will never come if Renee keeps asking him out first."

"I have an idea," Allie said. "This will cheer you up. Why don't the three of us go rollerblading this Saturday night!"

"Okay. That could be fun," Stephanie said.

"Great!" Allie replied.

"Poor Stephanie." Darcy was laughing. "Renee Salter *and* Comet's leftovers in the same day!"

"Well, at least I feel better about tomorrow," Stephanie said.

"What do you mean?" Darcy asked.

Stephanie grinned. "There's no way tomorrow could be any worse than today!"

CHAPTER
3

◆ ◄ ◆ ◆

Stephanie was in a better mood when she woke up the next day. It was early, and she was even the first one into the bathroom! She sneaked an extra minute onto her three-minutes-only shower.

There were strict rules about taking three-minute showers in the Tanner house. That was because there were so many people fighting to get into the bathroom. Besides Stephanie, Michelle, and their dad, there was Stephanie's older sister, D.J., who was always in a rush to get to her morning classes at a nearby college.

Then there was Joey Gladstone. Joey had moved in after Stephanie's mom died in a car accident eight years ago. Joey was a lot of fun, especially

14

when he did his impressions of famous cartoon characters. He sometimes did them on the radio show that he shared with Stephanie's uncle Jesse.

Jesse was also an important part of the family. So were his twin sons, Alex and Nicky. Stephanie adored her four-year-old cousins and their mom, Becky. Becky worked in television. She was a producer and co-host of the program *Wake Up, San Francisco*.

Stephanie's dad was the other host. It was a lot of fun having so many great people in one house— even if it usually meant fighting over the bathroom.

"All done in the shower!" Stephanie called as she raced back to her room to get dressed. She changed her mind twice before deciding to wear bright blue leggings and her favorite tie-dyed T-shirt. She grabbed a bagel and rushed out the door to catch the bus.

She was out of breath by the time she met Allie and Darcy at the pay phone by the gym.

"We've been dying for you to get here," Allie cried. "I have the best news!"

"The best news would be a surprise holiday," Stephanie joked. "So this must be the *second*-best news."

"I don't think so, Steph." Darcy grinned. "It's definitely the best."

Allie took a deep breath. "On the bus this morning I heard Cynthia Hanson—she's the new seventh-grade Flamingo—tell Leslie Brannigan that Renee asked Kyle to a party at her house on Friday night."

Stephanie gulped. "That's supposed to be good news?" She shook her head. "I thought you guys were my friends."

"We are!" Darcy cried.

"Kyle said *no!*" Allie practically shouted.

"As in no way, not a chance, uh-uh, no thanks," Darcy chanted.

"Okay, okay." Stephanie laughed. "I get the picture. But did you guys ever think of this—what if Kyle said no because he has plans with someone else?"

"He's not dating anyone else at John Muir," Darcy insisted. "Or we'd know about it."

"That's definitely true," Stephanie agreed. "But maybe he's dating someone from a different school."

"There's only one way to find out, Steph," Allie said.

"That's right." Darcy poked Stephanie in the ribs. "*You'll* have to ask him."

They walked past a knot of students on their

way to their lockers. Stephanie lowered her voice. "Are you kidding? After what happened yesterday?"

"Come on, Steph," Allie urged. "You have to do it. What if he told Renee no because he's waiting for a better invitation?"

"Like from *you*," Darcy added.

"No way," Stephanie cried as they turned a corner. "No way am I asking Kyle—"

"Asking me what?"

Stephanie stopped in her tracks. Kyle Sullivan was standing right in front of her.

"Kyle!" Stephanie swallowed hard.

"Ask him," Allie whispered.

"It's now or never, Steph," Darcy agreed.

"Did you want to ask me something?" Kyle stared at Stephanie.

"Oh . . . uh . . . yeah, I wanted to ask you about . . ." Stephanie hesitated. "About . . . about the paper!" she finally cried. "You know, the *Scribe*. We were thinking of doing some interviews with some of the sports team captains."

"Interviews?" Darcy and Allie both said. They exchanged an impatient glance.

"Right," Stephanie answered. She glared at them before turning back to Kyle. "Interviews. And since you're one of the captains of the soccer team, you're a perfect choice."

"Oh," Kyle said, looking a little surprised. "Well, sure. An interview would be fine, I guess."

"Okay," Stephanie replied. "I'll tell the editor." *Why did I say that?* She groaned to herself.

I can't believe I said I wanted to interview him! She started to move away.

"Wait, Steph," Kyle said. "What are you doing Friday night?"

"Friday night?" Stephanie repeated. "Um. Nothing on Friday. Let's see . . . Nope."

"Maybe we should do something together," Kyle said.

Stephanie stared at him with a blank expression. *He's asking me out!* she wanted to scream.

Hold on, hold on. Don't freak out. Don't blow it.

She could feel Darcy's fingers digging into her right arm. Allie's fingers were already buried in her left arm.

"Uh, great," Stephanie said. She hoped her voice didn't sound as shaky as she felt.

"Okay." Kyle nodded. "I'll call you."

Stephanie stood totally still. She watched Kyle turn and walk away down the hall. As soon as he rounded the corner she heard screaming in her ears.

Is that noise coming from me? she wondered. *Yes!*

"He asked you out!" Allie screeched. "Oh, wow, Steph, he *asked* you *out!*"

"He did! He really did!" Stephanie said.

"So you'll go out with Kyle on Friday and tell us *everything* about it on Saturday!" Darcy said.

"Sure," Stephanie replied. She felt slightly dazed. *My first big date,* she thought. She glanced around her. *I'll remember this hallway forever.* A grin spread over her face.

"You have a real date," Allie murmured with a dreamy look on her face.

"And not just any date," Darcy pointed out. "A date with Kyle Sullivan."

"Wait till the Flamingoes hear about this," Allie said.

Stephanie laughed at Allie. "And you thought you had the best news ever. But this is better. Kyle doesn't have a date with Renee on Friday . . . because he has a date with me!"

"I'm so impressed," Allie said. "You and Kyle Sullivan. And I *know* you. Wow."

The morning passed in a blur. Stephanie couldn't even remember going from one class to the next. Before she knew it, it was lunchtime. She was back in the cafeteria. Stephanie spotted Darcy and Allie sitting at their usual table. Some other eighth-grade girls were with them: Mackenzie Sant, Sue Kramer, and Kara Landford.

"Hey, guys," Stephanie said happily as she joined them.

"How was your morning?" Darcy asked.

"Great!" Stephanie reached into her lunch bag and pulled out a soggy tuna sandwich. *Tuna,* Stephanie thought. *This is the-day-Kyle-Sullivan-asked-me-on-a-date tuna. I'll remember this tuna forever!*

"I can see why you're happy," Kara said. She poked at the food on her tray. "You don't have to eat this goo."

"Yeah," Sue agreed, stirring a puddle of yellowy mush. "Today's lunch is even worse than yesterday's. And yesterday's was awful. It's a good thing you brought food from home."

"Speaking of food, I'm having a barbecue on Friday," Mackenzie said. "And you guys are all invited."

"Super," Darcy replied. "I love barbecues."

"Me too," Allie agreed.

"What about you, Steph?" Mackenzie asked.

"Friday?" Stephanie grinned. "I'd love to, but— I'm busy."

Darcy and Allie started giggling.

"You are?" Sue seemed surprised.

"Yeah, well—I sort of have a date," Stephanie added.

Mackenzie's eyes were bright with curiosity. "With who?" she asked. The whole table leaned toward Stephanie.

"She has a date with Kyle Sullivan!" Allie blurted. "Sorry, Steph, I couldn't help it," Allie apologized.

"Wow," Sue finally said. "He is so cool."

"*Ultra* cool," Kara agreed.

"Amazing," Mackenzie murmured.

They all stared at Stephanie with admiration. Stephanie felt great. She had a date with one of the most popular guys at school. And by tomorrow everyone in the eighth grade would know.

Things don't get any better than this, Stephanie thought.

Stephanie was so happy, she floated through the rest of her day. She loved every one of her classes. She loved the homework she got in math. She loved the bus ride home. She loved her house when she sailed through the front door. She even loved the smudge Comet left on her shirt when he jumped up to greet her.

"Good boy." Stephanie patted the big dog on the head.

D.J. was sitting on the couch, poring over some

old fashion magazines. She glanced up as Stephanie entered the room.

"Hello, wonderful sister," Stephanie called.

"Boy, Steph, you're sure in a great mood," D.J. remarked. "What happened? School burn down?"

"Nope." Stephanie grinned happily. "It's still there. Beautiful old John Muir."

"Did you say 'beautiful John Muir'?" D.J. laughed. "This *must* have something to do with a boy."

Stephanie shrugged, trying to seem casual. "It's no big deal. I just happen to have a date for Friday night."

"Oh, Stephanie!" D.J. jumped up and rushed to give Stephanie a hug. "That's so exciting! Your first real date!"

"A date?" Danny said, coming out of the kitchen. "Did I hear someone say something about a date?"

"Yes." Stephanie grinned. "I'm going on a date. This Friday."

"With a boy?" Danny raised his eyebrows.

"Of course. Come on, Dad," D.J. teased. "It had to be a boy. If Steph was doing something with Darcy and Allie, she would say *plans.* But *date* means only one thing."

"Do I know this boy?" Danny frowned.

"Sort of," Stephanie told him. "He's the one who sent me a valentine over the radio."

"Kyle Sullivan?" D.J. said. "That's great, Steph!"

"Yeah. And don't worry, Dad," Stephanie assured her father. "He's only the most gorgeous, most popular, most amazing guy in school." She paused. "Kyle Sullivan," she said in a dreamy voice.

"That's quite a description." Danny smiled.

"What are you planning to do on your first big date?" D.J. asked.

"I don't know yet," Stephanie said. "Something good, I hope."

"Well, I hope you find out soon," D.J. told her.

"Oh, I will. He said he's going to call," Stephanie replied. "I guess we'll talk about it then."

"Let me know if you need a ride anywhere," Danny said. "I'll be happy to take you. Or maybe you'll need a chaperone. You know it's not always safe for young people to be out on their own. I could always tag along—"

"No way, Dad!" Stephanie cried in horror.

"Don't worry, Steph. Dad tried to invite himself along on *my* first date, too." D.J. laughed.

Danny put his arm around Stephanie's shoulders. He smiled at her almost sadly. "I'm happy for you, honey. My little girl is growing up." Danny reached up to wipe a tear from his eye.

"Your first big date. You're becoming such a young lady. Maybe there are one or two things we should talk about—"

"Things?" Stephanie asked.

D.J. rolled her eyes. "I also got *that* speech on my first date," D.J. said. "I guess it's a Tanner family tradition. But just think, Stephanie. When it's over, Dad will only be able to use his speech one more time—on Michelle."

"Uh, love to hear your speech, Dad," Stephanie told him. "But I've got a ton of homework to do."

Stephanie escaped to her room. Danny didn't give her his speech. But there was lots of good-natured teasing about her big date at dinner.

Joey told about a hundred bad dating jokes. And Jesse told about two hundred stories about his wild dating life before he married Becky. D.J. got teary eyed talking about her first date.

"I don't know why everyone's so excited," Michelle complained. "Just because Stephanie wants to go out with a boy. Boys can be yucky. Especially the ones who try and kiss you."

The whole family hooted with laughter. Stephanie suddenly thought about Kyle kissing *her*. She felt her cheeks flush bright red.

"Uh, thanks, Michelle. I'd better go finish my

homework," Stephanie told them all. She raced back upstairs.

Actually her homework was almost done. What she really wanted to do was pick out a great outfit for the next day. She had to look her absolute best. After all, she might run into Kyle.

She tried out a dozen looks. Finally she settled on her blue-and-white pleated skirt. It would go great with her new chunky white sneakers. She would wear them both with her white baby tee. And she'd do her hair loose. Or maybe mostly loose, but with one thin braid on the side.

Stephanie stared at her hair in the mirror and frowned. She hadn't worn her hair in that style for a long time. She'd better try the braid tonight. She wanted to make sure it was the look she really wanted.

Stephanie lifted her hairbrush off her dresser. She ran it through her hair several times. Her hair looked smooth and fluffy and—

What is that? Stephanie thought in alarm.

Stephanie peered closer into the mirror. Her hair was orange!

What is going on? Stephanie quickly ran her fingers through her hair and shook her head. Orange stuff flew through the air. She glanced at her brush. Clumps of orange fuzz were stuck to the bristles.

Michelle came into the room to get ready for bed.

"Michelle," Stephanie said in a sweet voice. "Have you been using my hairbrush?"

"Nope," Michelle replied. "I have my own hairbrush."

"Then what is this?" Stephanie demanded. She pulled some orange fuzz out of her brush and waved it in Michelle's face.

"Oh. That's Lily the Lion's hair," Michelle said. "She doesn't have her own brush, so she borrowed yours."

"Michelle!" Stephanie cried. "You know you're not supposed to take my things! This is too much. Lately you've been breaking all the rules."

Before Michelle could answer, there was a knock at the door. Danny entered the room. "Time for bed," he announced. He gave Michelle a kiss good night. He crossed the room and ruffled Stephanie's hair.

"I hope you're not too old for a good-night kiss, Steph," he said. "Now that you're dating," he added.

Stephanie laughed. "Of course not, Dad." She raised her cheek and Danny kissed her good night also.

Danny left the room and Michelle climbed into her bed. She pulled the covers under her chin. "Lights out, please," she ordered Stephanie.

"But I haven't finished trying on my outfit yet," Stephanie protested.

"Sorry," Michelle told her. "You know that's Dad's rule. Lights out after I'm in bed."

Stephanie sighed. She would have to try on the skirt with her baby tee tomorrow. She reached out to turn off the light. Her arm brushed against something heavy. There was a loud noise as it clattered onto the floor.

"What was that?" Stephanie yelped. Her arm was all wet. Quickly she reached for the light and switched it back on.

"Oh, no," she moaned. "My homework! It's totally ruined."

Water had spilled all over her desk. The neat homework pages she'd finished were sitting in a puddle. She'd have to copy everything over again before she could hand it in.

"Michelle!" Stephanie cried. "Did you leave something full of water on my dresser?"

"Uh-oh." Michelle sat up in bed. "Do you see Timothy the Turtle anywhere?"

"Don't tell me that's turtle water!" Stephanie exclaimed. She glanced down at the floor. Timothy's glass bowl was lying on the rug.

Michelle leaped out of bed and hurried to Stephanie's side of the room. She searched under the furniture. "Timothy!" she called. Finally she found the turtle under Stephanie's bed. She placed him back in the bowl.

"That's it, Michelle!" Stephanie stamped her foot in anger. "You know that turtle's not supposed to be on my side of the room! Something's got to change around here. It's time to make the rules perfectly clear."

Stephanie grabbed a notebook and flipped to a blank page. She pulled a pen from her bag and started writing furiously.

"Okay," she said. She ripped the page from her notebook and pinned it up on her bulletin board with a thumbtack.

"These are the rules, Michelle," Stephanie announced. She crossed her arms over her chest and read out loud:

1. *No food in the bedroom.*
2. *No Comet in the bedroom.*
3. *No animals in bowls without lids.*
4. *No putting your stuff on my side of the room.*
5. *No locking the door.*
6. *No entering without knocking.*
7. *No stuffed animals on Stephanie's bed.*
8. *No radio on while homework is being done.*
9. *No borrowing clothes.*

10. *No using Stephanie's brush on anything, live or stuffed.*

"Got it?" Stephanie asked when she had finished reading.

"Okay," Michelle replied. "But you're breaking a rule right now."

"Which one is that?" Stephanie asked.

Michelle got back into her bed. "No lights on after Michelle's in bed," she replied. She pulled the covers up again and stared at the light switch on the wall.

"Fine," Stephanie snapped, flicking off the light.

Great, she thought. *But I still have to finish my homework.*

Stephanie stumbled over to her desk in the dark and grabbed her soggy homework. She banged her leg on her chair.

"Ow!" she yelped.

"Shh," Michelle whispered. "You're breaking the no-banging-around-the-room-after-Michelle's-bedtime rule."

"Yeah, and in another minute I'm going to break the no-strangling-Michelle rule," Stephanie shot back.

She stepped into the hall and slammed the door behind her. She was probably breaking the no-slamming-the-door-after-Michelle's-in-bed rule. But right now, she really didn't care.

CHAPTER
4

◆ ◀ ◆ ◆

Stephanie and Kyle were walking arm in arm through the halls at school. They gazed lovingly into each other's eyes. They had been together every minute since their big date. The halls were lined with kids who tossed flowers at them as they passed. It was so romantic. Even the lunchroom ladies were smiling and throwing flowers at them.

Kyle glanced down and patted Stephanie's shoulder. *Honey*, he called. *Honey!*

Honey, Stephanie repeated.

"Honey? Honey, wake up. You're going to be late for school."

"What?" Stephanie rubbed her eyes. It wasn't Kyle calling her honey. It was her dad. Danny was looking down at her with a worried look on his face.

"Steph? Are you okay? Are you sick? You look a little flushed. Are you feeling all right?"

I was dreaming! Stephanie realized. She smiled and pulled the blankets more tightly around her. *What an amazing dream!*

"Steph, shouldn't you be up by now?" Danny asked.

Stephanie sat up, suddenly wide awake. "What time is it, Dad?"

"Well," Danny said, checking his watch. "If you still want to take a shower, I'd say at this point the three-minute limit will seem very generous."

Stephanie turned to check her clock. Seven forty-five! She had exactly fifteen minutes to get to the bus.

"Thanks, Dad!" Stephanie leaped from the bed and raced past her father to the bathroom. Luckily D.J. was just coming out.

Stephanie set a new speed record. She was in and out of the bathroom in under two minutes.

She raced back into her room. No time now for the special mini-braid in her hair. She brushed it as quickly as she could and left it loose.

Now, where is that blue-and-white skirt?

Oh, yeah—she had hung it in the front of her

closet so it wouldn't get wrinkled. She pulled on the pleated skirt. It looked great. She yanked on her new white sneakers. All she needed now was that cute white baby tee. She hadn't been able to look for it the night before.

She yanked open her middle dresser drawer. The T-shirt wasn't on top where she thought it might be. She sifted through everything in the drawer. No tee.

Stephanie frowned. *I know it was in here,* she thought. She pulled out her other dresser drawers. One by one she searched through them. Still no white baby tee. Where was it?

She glanced around the room and groaned. Clothes were strewn all over the floor. Michelle came into the room to grab her backpack for school.

"Michelle," Stephanie said. "You have to pick up your dirty laundry! How can a person find anything in this mess?"

"Is that another rule?" Michelle asked.

"Yes," Stephanie told her. "It's another rule."

"I think that's too many rules to remember," Michelle replied.

"Michelle . . ." Stephanie warned her.

"Those aren't even my dirty clothes," Michelle

said. "They're your clean clothes. You must have kicked them off the bed last night."

"What?" Stephanie took a closer look at the pile of clothes. Michelle was right.

"Isn't there a rule against kicking clothes off your bed?" Michelle asked. She walked to the list of rules and peered at them.

"Of course not," Stephanie said. She stooped down and started searching through the clothes on the floor. "You can't follow a rule if you're asleep."

She searched through the whole pile. Still no T-shirt.

"Michelle, have you seen my white baby tee? Stephanie asked."

"Nope," Michelle replied.

Stephanie thought Michelle had a guilty look on her face. "Because if you borrowed it without asking, you'll be breaking a rule," Stephanie warned. "And you'll have to do one of my chores as punishment—like walking Comet for me or folding the laundry."

"Really? Same for you?" Michelle asked.

"Sure," Stephanie replied. "Rules are rules, and we both have to follow them."

Like I'm ever going to borrow your clothes in this lifetime, Stephanie thought.

"Okay," Michelle said.

"Well?" Stephanie stood there, her hand on her hip.

"Well, what?" Michelle asked.

"Well, I'm in a hurry. So where's my baby tee?"

"I don't know," Michelle answered. "But I have to leave now or I'll be late for school. Good luck."

Stephanie sighed and turned back to the room. It looked like a disaster area. And the T-shirt wasn't anywhere. Michelle *must* have taken it. Stephanie checked the clock. She was really running late. If she didn't leave in the next sixty seconds, she'd even miss the late bus to school.

What's that? Something white peeked out from under Michelle's pillow.

"Stephanie!" Danny called from downstairs. "You've got three seconds to leave!"

Stephanie raced across the room. She snatched up Michelle's pillow. Her white baby tee lay underneath!

"I knew she had it!" Stephanie cried. She yanked the shirt over her head. She grabbed her backpack and rushed down the stairs. She pulled on her denim jacket and ran into the kitchen. She had just enough time to grab a bagel before dashing out the door.

"Boy, you're cutting it close," Joey called out, checking his watch as Stephanie flew by.

My first day at school as a girl with a date, Stephanie thought. *And I have no idea what I look like!*

Luckily Stephanie made the bus. But just barely. And by the time she met Darcy and Allie at the pay phone, they had only a few minutes to talk.

"So how does it feel?" Allie asked. Her eyes were shining with excitement and a little envy.

"How does what feel?" Stephanie asked, pretending not to understand.

"How does it feel to be a girl who has Friday-night plans with the cutest boy in school?" Darcy answered for her.

"Oh, that," Stephanie said. "Hmmm. I don't know," she said, pretending to think about it. "It feels great!" she burst out.

Darcy giggled.

Allie sighed. "I always think that I'd feel totally different if I had a special date."

"I was in such a rush this morning," Stephanie told them. "I didn't get to enjoy the idea too much. But—" She lowered her voice. "I did dream about Kyle last night."

"Oh, that's so romantic!" Allie cried.

"Now the big question is: Did he dream about *you?*" Darcy teased. Her hazel eyes danced with mischief. "Maybe we should ask him."

"I dare you," Stephanie joked back. The three girls made their way to their lockers.

"I will ask him," Darcy said. "Because—here comes Kyle!"

Stephanie felt butterflies in her stomach. She felt excited and nervous all at the same time. She whirled around, prepared to face Kyle.

Ooops! Darcy forgot to mention one small detail. Kyle was with Renee Salter. Renee was wearing pink leggings tucked into short black boots, her own baby tee, and a flowered vest. Stephanie had to admit Renee looked amazing.

But today I don't even care, Stephanie realized. *Don't forget,* she told herself. You're *the one he has a date with.*

Stephanie turned around just long enough to take off her jacket and throw it in her locker. She took a deep breath and turned around again.

"Hi, Ky—" she began. She stopped. Kyle and Renee were staring at her curiously. Renee pointed to Stephanie's T-shirt. She started howling with laughter.

Stephanie noticed that Allie and Darcy were staring at her shirt too.

Did I spill something on myself? Stephanie wondered. *Oh, please, not on my favorite baby tee.*

Stephanie glanced down.

"Oh, no!" Stephanie cried. She flung her arms over her chest.

Tell me this isn't happening.

She wasn't wearing *her* baby tee. She was wearing Michelle's T-shirt. And it was decorated with a big, bright picture of the Troll family.

"Oh, Steph, that's so cute!" Renee cried, loudly enough for everyone in the hall to stop and look. "Trolls! The little girl I *baby-sit* has a shirt just like that."

Stephanie was mortified.

"The Troll family!" Renee chuckled. "Really, Steph. That's just so . . . *cute.*"

There was nothing Stephanie could do. She dropped her arms and tried to smile. "Yeah. You've got to love those trolls," she muttered.

Kyle grinned and shook his head. "Hey, Steph, don't forget about Friday night," he said. "We're still on, right?"

"Right," Stephanie managed to say.

The expression on Renee's face made Stephanie feel a little better. Renee looked totally shocked.

"By the way," Stephanie added. "We haven't decided what we're going to do."

"I'll call and let you know," Kyle said.

"Oh," Stephanie replied. "Because I was thinking of, maybe, rollerblading, or—"

"Come *on*, Kyle," Renee interrupted. "We'll be late for homeroom."

"Okay, sure," Kyle answered. "Bye, Steph."

Before Stephanie could even nod, Kyle was gone. She gazed after Kyle and Renee as they disappeared into the crowded hall.

"Renee is so pushy," Allie complained. "Did you see the way she purposely cut you off? Obviously she didn't want you to plan anything with Kyle."

"She's just jealous," Darcy added. "Her jaw practically hit the floor when Kyle mentioned your date on Friday night."

"Well, I hope you do something great," Allie said. "Does Kyle like rollerblading?"

"I don't know." Stephanie shrugged. "I guess I won't know anything until he calls."

"How can you stand not knowing?" Allie wondered. "I'd be going crazy. A major date in only two days. And you don't know what you're doing!"

"Yeah," Darcy agreed. "How can you plan what to wear?"

Stephanie had to admit she agreed with her friends. After all, this was going to be the date of her dreams. And she still didn't have a clue what the date would be.

CHAPTER
5

♦ ◄ ▪ ♦

"Hey, Steph," Carrie Dunbar whispered. "Aren't you hot in that heavy sweatshirt?"

Stephanie shifted in her chair and smiled weakly. "I'm fine. It was pretty chilly in here."

Actually Stephanie was boiling hot. Darcy had loaned her a sweatshirt to wear over the troll T-shirt. Stephanie was glad no one else had seen the embarrassing picture. But she'd be even more glad when classes were over and she could take the sweatshirt off.

"Okay, everyone, listen up." Ms. Trent, Stephanie's social studies teacher, stood at the front of the room. A list of women's names was written on the blackboard behind her.

"I want you to tell me anything you know about each of these people," she said. "First off, Amelia Earhart."

"Didn't she fly a plane?" Cindi Wang asked.

"Yeah," Jenni Gordon agreed. "But she wasn't such a good pilot. Not like that guy who flew around the world. She got lost!"

"She didn't get lost," Laurie Lewis corrected her. "She disappeared. No one ever found her or her plane. I saw a show about it on television."

"Good enough," Ms. Trent said. "What about Susan B. Anthony?"

Stephanie knew something about her. "They made a dollar coin with her picture on it," Stephanie said. "My dad is keeping some of the first coins they made for me and my two sisters."

Ms. Trent cleared her throat. "Do you know anything about what Susan B. Anthony did before she was on the dollar coin?" she asked.

All anyone knew was that people always confused the dollar coins with quarters.

"Well, Susan B. Anthony led the fight for women's rights. She was very famous early in this century. How about Rosie the Riveter?" Ms. Trent asked.

That one stumped the whole class. Greg Washington raised his hand.

"What's a rivet anyway?" he asked.

Ms. Trent laughed. "A rivet is a metal fastener. They're shot out of special tools. They were once used to build machinery—and airplanes. Rosie the Riveter was a nickname for the thousands of women who worked in factories during World War Two. The men were soldiers, so the women took over the jobs that men had always done before, even building airplanes!"

"Cool," Greg murmured.

"Very cool," Ms. Trent agreed. She pointed to another name on the blackboard. "Wilma Rudolph was a famous African-American athlete. She was the first American woman to win a gold medal in Olympic track and field," she said.

It turned out that no one really knew much about any of the names on Ms. Trent's list.

"We're starting a section on women's history next," the teacher announced.

The boys in the class groaned. The girls scowled at them.

"All of these women changed history," Ms. Trent told the class. "And now you see why it's important to know about them. Women like these changed our lives because of what they did."

"How could they?" Greg asked. "They've all

been dead for about a hundred years, haven't they?"

Everyone laughed. Ms. Trent smiled.

"That's a good question, Greg," she said. "Actually you may not realize this, but women only won the right to vote in 1920."

A low murmur filled the class. Stephanie was amazed too. What would life be like in her house if only her dad, Jesse, and Joey made all the decisions?

"We really have come a long way," Stephanie commented. "Now there are women who are senators and representatives."

"And maybe someday we'll have a woman president, too," Ms. Trent added. Some of the boys moaned again.

"Your homework tonight is to think about the changing roles of women—and men—throughout the history of this country," Ms. Trent said. "Who changed the roles men and women have? What other changes would be helpful, or even harmful? I'll want an essay from each of you on Monday."

What a great topic! Stephanie thought in excitement. Maybe she would pick a famous female author to write about!

After class Stephanie hurried to meet Darcy and

Allie by their lockers. She peeled off the sweatshirt and breathed a sigh of relief.

"That's better," she said. "I felt like I was going to pass out." She handed the sweatshirt back to Darcy. "But thanks for the loan."

"No problem," Darcy replied. She tossed the sweatshirt back into her locker and grabbed her book bag. "I'm glad I never got around to taking it home."

"Maybe Steph should wear it on her date," Allie joked.

"Yeah. Maybe Kyle will take you to a freezing cold ice rink," Darcy teased.

"Very funny," Stephanie said. Still, it was kind of hard not to know where she was going.

"When Kyle said he'd call, I hope he meant to-night," Darcy said. "It's already Wednesday. You should have *at least* two full days to figure out your outfit."

Stephanie nodded. "I hope he calls tonight too."

"Why don't you just call him when you get home?" Allie suggested. "You two really need a chance to talk about it."

"Why don't you go to the big street fair?" Darcy suggested. "That would be fun. They always have tons of great kinds of food. I think they're going to have some games this year, too."

"Or you could see the new Keanu Reeves movie," Allie said. "I'd love to see that on a date. It looks really romantic."

"I don't know." Stephanie shrugged. "Those ideas both sound like fun. But Kyle did say *he'd* call *me*. I don't want to bug him about it. He'll think I've never been on a date before."

"Steph, you haven't," Darcy pointed out.

"Yeah," Stephanie admitted. "But that's no reason to act like I haven't. I need to be cool with someone like Kyle."

"And you need to *look* cool," Darcy agreed. "Which brings us back to the clothing situation. Maybe you can borrow something from D.J."

"No way," Stephanie said. "D.J. never lets me borrow her clothes."

"But this is different. It's your first big date," Allie pointed out.

"True," Stephanie said. "Even D.J. might break her rule for this."

CHAPTER
6

◆ ◀ ◗ ◆

Stephanie rushed straight to D.J.'s room the minute she got home. No time was a good time to ask D.J. to lend clothes. So Stephanie figured she should get it over with sooner rather than later.

Stephanie poked her head into her sister's room. "Hey, Deej," she said sweetly. "Are you studying for a test or something? Is there anything I can get you? Cookies, a soda?"

"Okay." D.J. sighed. She closed the textbook she'd been reading. "What do you want to borrow?"

Stephanie grinned. "Anything!"

"Wait a minute," D.J. said. She peered more closely at Stephanie. "Why are you wearing Michelle's T-shirt? Is that a new style or something?"

"Yeah," Stephanie said. "Looking like a nine-year-old is very hot right now."

"I'm not going to lend you my clothes. Not if you're going to wear them with Michelle's clothes," D.J. joked. "It's either me or her. College and third-grade fashions just do not mix."

"Don't worry," Stephanie replied. "This was a mistake never to be repeated." She explained what had happened with Kyle and Renee at school.

"That's tough," D.J. said with sympathy. "So what do you want to try on?" She smiled. "What are you and Kyle doing, anyway?"

"I'm not sure," Stephanie admitted. "Kyle is supposed to call me and let me know."

"Well, we'll pick something good for any kind of date," D.J. promised.

Stephanie leaned into D.J.'s closet. "Ooh!" she cried. "How about this?" She held up a black knitted cardigan D.J. had gotten recently. It had three-quarter-length sleeves and amazingly cool stone buttons. Best of all, it was knitted in an openwork pattern that looked like lace. Stephanie held it against her.

D.J. bit her lip. 'Well, that's one of my newest things," she said. "But . . ."

"Oh, please, please, pretty please," Stephanie

begged. She admired herself in the mirror on D.J.'s door.

"For your first big date, okay," D.J. agreed. "But don't think you can make a habit of it."

"Thanks!" Stephanie cried. She flung her arms around D.J.'s neck.

"Okay, okay, don't kill me for it." D.J. grinned.

"No matter what we do, this will be perfect," Stephanie said. *And it will look fabulous with my real baby tee,* she thought. *If I ever find it, that is.*

The phone rang. Stephanie's heart stopped for a second.

I hope it's Kyle, she thought.

D.J. answered before anyone else could pick up. She covered the mouthpiece with her hand.

"It's Kyle," she whispered. "He has a nice voice."

"Uh, Deej?" Stephanie asked. "Could you do me one more favor?"

D.J. raised her eyebrow.

"Could I have some privacy?" Stephanie asked.

"Okay," D.J. said. "You can use my room. But don't stay on the phone long. I've got to make a call too."

Stephanie grabbed the phone. "Thank you, thank you," she whispered.

"Five minutes," D.J. warned as she stepped out the door.

Stephanie took a deep breath. Then she raised the receiver to her ear.

"Kyle?" she asked.

"Hey, Stephanie," Kyle said.

He *did* have a nice voice.

"It's great that you called now," Stephanie told him. "I was just thinking about what we could do on Friday—"

"I have a great plan," Kyle interrupted.

"Oh," Stephanie said in surprise. "Because I was thinking—"

"Don't worry. Here's what we'll do," Kyle began. "I'll pick you up at seven thirty. We'll go to the mall and have Chinese food. After that I thought we could see the new Tom Cruise movie. My brother will pick us up at eleven and you'll be home by eleven thirty."

"Oh. Well, great," Stephanie managed to say.

Wow, I sound like a jerk, she thought. "I mean, I didn't expect you to have everything planned."

"I'm a great planner," Kyle said. "You know, I've done this before."

"Oh," Stephanie said. "I guess you didn't need any help, then."

"Nope." Kyle laughed. "I'll see you Friday."

Kyle hung up. Stephanie stood staring at the phone for a minute. She wasn't sure how she felt. Kyle had already planned their whole date. She'd been looking forward to suggesting the street fair. Or maybe the new Christian Slater movie.

Still, it was kind of cool that Kyle had taken the trouble to figure out the whole date by himself. Stephanie checked her watch.

Their conversation had lasted only about thirty seconds. She had four and a half minutes left. She decided to call Darcy and Allie.

Stephanie dialed Allie, and in a few seconds they had Darcy on the phone too. Stephanie told them about the date Kyle had planned.

"I thought you wanted to see the Keanu Reeves movie," Allie said.

"That's the movie *you* wanted to see, Allie," Darcy reminded her.

Stephanie laughed. "Actually I'd rather see the Christian Slater movie. But any movie with Kyle is better than no movie with Kyle."

"I guess that's true," Darcy agreed. "But there is one tiny problem. Don't you have the same curfew as me—ten o'clock? Can you really stay out until eleven thirty?"

"I don't know," Stephanie admitted. She'd thought of her curfew while Kyle was talking. But he hadn't given her a chance to say anything. And besides, what would she have said?

Sorry, Kyle, I'll have to check with my father before I say yes? That would have made a great impression.

Stephanie sighed. "I'll have to ask my dad. I just hope he says yes."

Stephanie suddenly felt sick to her stomach. "No way I'm going to tell Kyle I can't go. What if he decides to ask Renee instead? I bet she doesn't have a ten o'clock curfew."

"You could always find a different movie," Allie said. "An earlier one that you both want to see."

"I know," Stephanie replied. "It's just that he went to a lot of trouble to plan it all."

Even if he didn't ask my opinion, she thought. She shook her head. It wasn't fair to think that.

"At least you know what you're doing," Darcy said. "Hmmm . . . a long skirt could be perfect for a movie date."

"Good idea," Stephanie agreed. "My yellow flowered skirt would look great with the sweater I just borrowed from D.J.!"

Stephanie said good night to her friends and hung up the phone. At least she could pick out the perfect outfit now. She burst into her room without knocking.

"Uh-oh, Stephanie. You broke a rule." Michelle

was sitting on her bed, having a tea party with some of her stuffed animals. "Rule number six," Michelle pointed out. "Knock before entering."

"I know, Michelle, but I forgot," Stephanie explained. "I've got some very important stuff to do now. So don't bother me."

"Well, I've got important stuff to do too," Michelle insisted. "Like loading the dishwasher after dinner."

"So?" Stephanie said. She hunted through her closet for her long yellow skirt.

"So you're going to do it for me," Michelle told her.

"But Michelle, I can't do your chore tonight," Stephanie started to protest. "You're not doing anything important like I am. I have to get ready for my date."

Michelle shook her head. "Those are the rules," she said in a stubborn voice. "You said it yourself—rules are rules."

Stephanie was about to argue. But she clamped her mouth shut. She *was* the one who'd written up the rules. She'd just have to pick out her perfect outfit later—after she'd done Michelle's chore.

Stephanie stayed in the kitchen after dinner. She helped clean up and then she began Michelle's chore. She loaded the dishwasher, trying to think of the best way to ask her father about her curfew. Finally she decided to plunge right in.

Her dad was leaning into the sink. He wore pink rubber gloves and he was rubbing special cleanser into the lasagna pan left over from dinner. Maybe he was too busy to pay attention.

"Dad, I've got to ask you something," she began.

"Ask away," Danny said.

"Remember my date on Friday?" Stephanie asked.

"Uh-huh," Danny said, leaning into the pan.

"Well, Kyle called me, and he's planned out a whole date. We're going to the mall to see the new Tom Cruise movie. It's supposed to be pretty good," she said.

"Great, honey." Danny nodded. "Do you need me to drive?"

"No, that's okay," Stephanie said quickly. "His brother will drive us."

"How old is this brother? Is he a safe driver?" Danny asked, looking over his shoulder at Stephanie. "Has he got seat belts for everyone in the car?"

"I'm sure he does, Dad," Stephanie assured him. "But there's just one little thing." Stephanie took a deep breath. She said the rest in a rush. "The movie is pretty long. It won't get out until eleven, but I'll be home by eleven thirty sharp."

"Wait a minute." Danny dropped the sponge.

Uh-oh, Stephanie thought. *Bad idea. Dad's never too busy to worry about curfews.*

"Did you say eleven thirty?" Danny asked.

"Yes," Stephanie admitted.

"I'm sorry, honey." Danny shook his head. "But you know your curfew is ten. No later."

"But Dad, Kyle is a ninth grader. He gets to stay out much later than me. Please let me stay out late just this once," Stephanie pleaded.

"Sorry, Steph," Danny replied. "A rule is a rule."

"But what am I going to tell him?" Stephanie moaned.

"Tell him the truth," Danny suggested. "I'm sure you can find an earlier movie."

"I know an earlier movie," Michelle announced as she came into the kitchen. *"The Mermaid's Garden*. It's supposed to be great. And it gets out way before your curfew."

"Thanks but no thanks, Michelle," Stephanie grumbled.

Danny glanced from Michelle to Stephanie to the dishwasher and back again. "That reminds me,

Stephanie—why are you loading the dishwasher? Isn't that Michelle's job tonight?"

"Sure, it's my job," Michelle began, "but Stephanie broke—"

"Broke her promise never to help her sister," Stephanie said quickly. "Michelle, why don't you go upstairs and do your homework? I'll finish up in here."

"That's a good idea, Michelle." Danny smiled.

"Okay," Michelle said. She left the kitchen.

Stephanie breathed a sigh of relief. The last thing she needed was for Michelle to blab that Stephanie had broken her own rules. That wouldn't exactly help her get a later curfew.

She glanced up at her father and was surprised to find him beaming at her.

"Stephanie, I'm impressed," Danny said proudly. "I think what you're doing is wonderful."

"What's wonderful?" Stephanie asked, feeling confused.

"Why, encouraging Michelle to do her schoolwork," Danny replied. "And helping her with her chores to give her time to do it."

"Oh, that," Stephanie said. "Of course." She thought quickly. Maybe she could convince her father that she was responsible enough to stay out later?

"Actually, I think it's my responsibility as an older sister," Stephanie told her dad. "I like to give Michelle some help when I can."

"That's a great attitude," Danny said.

Stephanie nodded. She was about ready to ask Danny for a later curfew. "You know, helping Michelle makes me feel more responsible in general," she added. "It's a great feeling."

"I agree." Danny's smile grew wider.

"I think it's every person's responsibility to help other people in the family when they need it," Stephanie finished. "Don't you?"

"I sure do!" Stephanie's uncle Jesse was standing in the kitchen doorway. He had a squirming twin under each arm. "I could sure use some help with these little guys."

Stephanie gulped. "What kind of help?"

"Well, Becky's out and I've got a ton of stuff to do before my radio show tomorrow," Jesse told her. "Could you read to the twins and put them to bed? I'd really appreciate it."

"Uh, well . . ." Stephanie didn't know what to say. There was no way she could say no. Not after everything she'd just told her father. Maybe if she did it, Danny would see how helpful she was being?

"Sure, Uncle Jesse." Stephanie forced a smile. At

this rate she'd be doing everyone's chores before she went to sleep.

"That's really generous of you, sweetie," Danny said.

"Yeah, Steph," Jesse agreed. "Thanks!"

"No problem." Stephanie smiled weakly. "Glad to help out." She took Nicky and Alex by their hands.

"Good night, honey," Danny said as Stephanie walked the twins to the door.

"Um, Dad." Stephanie gave it one last try. "About my curfew?"

"Ten o'clock, Stephanie." Danny smiled. "You know the rule."

I sure do, Stephanie thought. *The rule says I have to be home by ten. But what is my date going to say?*

CHAPTER
7

◆ ◀ ▪ ◆

Stephanie read stories to the twins until her throat was sore. Finally they fell asleep. Stephanie dashed downstairs and grabbed the portable phone. She dialed Allie's number and settled onto the couch.

"Allie! It's me. I have a crisis. I need to talk to both of you guys." Stephanie waited while Allie called Darcy on her three-way calling.

"What is it, Steph?" Darcy asked.

"My curfew." Stephanie moaned. "My dad said no way to staying out past ten!"

"Uh-oh," Allie said.

"What are you going to tell Kyle?" Darcy asked.

"That's the problem," Stephanie cried. "I *can't* tell him. I can't tell an older guy I have a curfew!

He'll wonder why he asked me out in the first place."

"He asked you out because he likes you," Allie reminded her.

"Yeah, but he might not if I start making changes. I told you how he planned everything out," Stephanie said. "I don't want him to ask out someone else instead of me."

"But you have a date," Allie protested. "He can't ask out someone else. Can he?" she asked.

"Sure, he can," Stephanie answered. "People break dates all the time. There aren't any rules, are there?"

"Well, there should be," Allie replied. "And the first one is that you can't cancel a date because of a curfew."

"Okay, that should be the rule," Darcy said. "But Steph has to do something about this now."

"You have to tell Kyle," Allie said.

"I know," Stephanie replied. "I just wish I said something when he called."

"It sounds like he hardly gave you a chance to think about your date," Darcy reminded her.

"That's true," Stephanie admitted.

"Will you tell him tomorrow?" Darcy asked.

"I guess I'll have to," Stephanie said. "I just hope he doesn't decide to ask Renee out instead."

Stephanie said good night to her friends and hung up the phone. What a disaster! She finally got a date with a boy she really liked, and now she had to change it.

She could just imagine how it was going to sound: *Sorry, Kyle. I know you've planned this excellent date. But eleven thirty is way past my bedtime.*

Stephanie cringed. It was going to be terrible. Kyle would probably think taking her to the movies was like . . . like her taking Michelle to see *The Mermaid's Garden.*

Becky came into the living room. "Stephanie, I want to thank you for helping with the boys tonight."

"That's okay," Stephanie replied.

"Steph?" Becky sat next to Stephanie on the couch. "Why the long face? You've been in such a good mood lately. Don't you still have your big date on Friday?"

"I think I have a date," Stephanie began. "I mean, I have a date, but I can't go on it."

"You lost me," Becky said.

"Kyle picked a movie for our date. But it doesn't get out until way after my curfew," Stephanie explained.

"Well, couldn't you find another movie?" Becky asked gently.

Stephanie lowered her eyes, feeling uncomfortable. "But he had the whole thing planned," Stephanie said. "He doesn't even know I have a curfew."

"I'm sure you two can work it out," Becky said. "Just remember, it takes two to make a date."

"There *is* another movie I'd rather see," Stephanie admitted.

"Don't be afraid to tell Kyle about it. I'm sure he wants to do what you want to do," Becky advised. "Otherwise, what kind of date will it be?"

"I was just so excited that he even asked me out," Stephanie said. "And when he told me the plans, he sounded so organized. I was impressed."

"That's nice sometimes," Becky agreed. "But you also have to speak up for yourself. You don't usually have that problem."

Stephanie laughed. "Not usually. But I don't usually have a date with the most popular boy in the ninth grade, either."

"I know." Becky smiled. "This is very special and exciting. I'm sure you want it to be perfect. But you have to stand up for yourself. We women need to say what we want, too."

Like Rosie the Riveter, Stephanie thought. *And Susan B. Anthony.*

Becky laughed. "If I never spoke up for what I

wanted, I might not be your aunt Becky. I asked Jesse on as many dates as he asked me."

"Really?" Stephanie asked.

"Sure." Becky lowered her voice "But don't tell him I told you. He likes to think he did it all himself."

Stephanie ran up to her bedroom, thinking about her conversation with Becky. What Becky said made sense. But Stephanie knew there was a big difference between thinking something and doing it. It was easy for Becky to give advice about guys. She was already married and had two little kids. Her last date must have been about a hundred years ago.

Stephanie still hadn't finished picking out the Big Movie Date Outfit. And she hadn't even started her social studies assignment.

Michelle glanced up as Stephanie entered the room. "Hey, is that my shirt?" Michelle's finger aimed at Stephanie's chest.

Ooops, Stephanie thought. *How am I going to explain this?*

"You didn't ask if you could borrow that," Michelle said.

"I know, Michelle," Stephanie told her. "But I was running late this morning. I made a mistake.

I thought it was *my* T-shirt. Besides, you weren't planning on wearing it."

"You still broke the rules," Michelle insisted. "So you have to do another one of my chores." Michelle thought for a moment. "You can walk Comet tomorrow."

"But Michelle . . ." Stephanie began.

"Rule number nine," Michelle insisted. "No borrowing clothes. You walk Comet."

Stephanie bit her tongue. She couldn't waste time arguing with a nine-year-old. She had important things to do. Like dream about her date. And start her essay on a woman who changed history. She would worry about chores tomorrow.

Stephanie sighed. *I hope I'm a famous woman myself someday,* she thought. *But I'll bet Susan B. Anthony and Rosie the Riveter didn't start their careers by walking the dog!*

"So—did you talk to Kyle yet?" Allie asked.

It was after school the next day. Stephanie had rushed to meet her friends by the pay phone.

Stephanie shook her head. "No. This Kyle situation is getting worse and worse."

"But Stephanie, it's already Thursday afternoon," Darcy said. "Your date is tomorrow night. Don't tell me you still haven't told him about your curfew." She frowned. "You better tell him—and fast."

"I know, I know," Stephanie muttered. So far, having a date with Kyle hadn't been as much fun as she'd thought. She was totally anxious about what was going to happen on Friday.

"What about lunchtime?" Allie said. "Kyle was there. I thought you were going to tell him about your curfew then."

Stephanie sighed. "How could I tell him? You saw Renee at lunch—she was all over him. I couldn't exactly walk up and tell Kyle about my curfew in front of her."

"Yeah," Darcy agreed. "If she knew you couldn't stay out late, she'd probably offer to go with Kyle instead." She giggled.

"Don't laugh—it's true," Stephanie told her. "I'll bet Renee is just waiting for something to go wrong with me and Kyle."

"So what are you going to do?" Allie asked.

"Well, I do have one plan," Stephanie answered. "I checked the paper and we *could* go to the new Christian Slater movie. It starts at eight and gets out at nine forty—just enough time to get home by ten."

"Sounds great!" Allie said. She smiled at Stephanie. "See? I knew you'd find a way to work things out. Well, I have to get home for my piano lesson," she added. "Let me know what happens."

Stephanie and Darcy waved good-bye to Allie.

"Hey, Steph, you can come over to my house if you want," Darcy offered.

"Thanks. But I can't," Stephanie answered. She pushed her long blond hair from her shoulders. "I have to get home—to walk the dog."

Darcy cocked her head. "I thought that was Michelle's job now."

"It is," Stephanie admitted. "I usually walk Comet on the weekends. But I have to do it for Michelle today since I wore her shirt yesterday."

"You're kidding!" Darcy started laughing. "Wasn't wearing her silly troll shirt like a punishment already?"

"It was," Stephanie agreed. "But I wrote the no-borrowing-clothes rule. And I broke it. So I had to pay by doing one of Michelle's chores for her."

"Boy, am I glad I don't have to follow your rules," Darcy said.

"Tell me about it," Stephanie replied.

"Hey, you two!"

Stephanie and Darcy both turned around. Stephanie's mouth dropped open. Kyle!

He was coming out of the gym with a sports

bag slung over his shoulder. Kyle looked terrific in a white T-shirt, loose gray shorts, and soccer shoes.

Breathe, Stephanie reminded herself. Kyle really was the cutest guy in school. Even when he was dressed for soccer practice!

"You guys are always hanging around that phone," Kyle joked. "Got some important calls to make?"

"Well, actually, I was thinking of calling you," Stephanie joked back. She and Darcy exchanged a glance.

"Tell him," Darcy whispered. She turned around and pretended to read a notice hanging by the door to the gym. Stephanie cleared her throat.

"Uh, see, Kyle—" Stephanie stopped. She wasn't sure how to start.

"Were you really thinking of calling me?" Kyle asked "Why?"

"Uh, about our date," Stephanie began.

"Really? What about it?" Kyle asked. He seemed suddenly worried.

"Well, I sort of forgot to tell you something last night." Stephanie knew she was blushing, but she couldn't help it. "I can't see the movie you picked out," she finally blurted.

"Why not?" Kyle asked. "What's wrong with Tom Cruise? You don't like him or something?"

Stephanie shook her head. "Of course I like him," she answered quickly.

"So what's wrong?" Kyle repeated.

"It's just that it gets out too late," Stephanie said. "The truth is, I have to be home by ten." *There. I said it! Now he knows the truth.* Stephanie definitely felt better. But what would Kyle say?

Kyle was frowning. "I wish you'd told me before," he said.

"Sorry," Stephanie muttered. She wanted to crawl under a rock and hide.

He probably thinks it was a mistake to ask me out in the first place, she told herself.

"Well, I'll check the paper and figure something out," Kyle finally told her.

Stephanie let out a sigh of relief. The date was still on!

"There is another movie we could see," Stephanie began. "This Christian Slater one—"

"I said I'll find something," Kyle interrupted. "And I'll still pick you up at seven thirty." Before Stephanie could reply, he turned around and went back into the gym.

"Did he hear a word you said?" Darcy asked.

Stephanie shrugged. "I guess I'll find out tomorrow night."

Darcy frowned at her. "This isn't like you, Stephanie. You didn't even tell Kyle how much you wanted to see that movie. Now he's just going to pick another movie that *he* wants to see."

"I know," Stephanie said in a quiet voice. *I hate to admit it*, she told herself. *But Darcy is right. I'm not being myself. And my big dream date is turning out to be one big problem.*

CHAPTER
8

◆ ◀ ▰ ◆

"Have fun tonight, Stephanie," Joey said. He sat at the kitchen table, spreading butter and garlic on his French bread. "Don't worry if you run out of things to say. Just tell him the joke about the dog that goes to the movies. I'll tell it right now so you'll remember. See, there's this big dog—"

"Please, don't tell me," Stephanie moaned. "After hearing it a hundred times, how could I forget it?"

Joey Gladstone was her dad's friend who lived with the Tanners. He was also a stand-up comic, and Stephanie's family had to listen to all the dumb jokes he liked to tell. And he usually told the same ones over and over.

"Stephanie never runs out of things to talk about," D.J. told Joey. "In fact, Kyle will probably be begging her to *stop* talking by the end of the night."

"Deej!" Stephanie cried in dismay.

"You'll have a great time," Becky assured Stephanie. She set a huge bowl of salad on the table.

It was Friday evening, and Stephanie was only thirty minutes away from her date. She hadn't been able to think of anything else all day.

In twelve hours I'll be in a car with Kyle and his brother. That was the first thing Stephanie had thought when she woke up.

At lunch it was, *Just seven hours and I'll be eating dinner with Kyle.*

After school she had thought, *Kyle is coming to pick me up in four and a half hours.*

Now it was, *One hour and I'll be sitting in the movies—next to Kyle—in the dark!*

Stephanie's stomach started doing flip-flops. Darcy and Allie had given her an hour-long pep talk. They gave her every bit of advice they could think of. Most of it boiled down to "relax" or "be yourself."

Stephanie thought that was excellent advice. But she was still nervous. What was their date going to be like? Would Kyle hold open doors for her? Would he do any really romantic stuff?

"Watch out!" Becky called. "It's hot." She set a huge platter of steaming spaghetti and meatballs on the table.

"I'm going out and you're all having one of my favorite meals," Stephanie complained. "Only kidding," she added.

"Well, sweetheart," Danny said. "You're welcome to stay here. You can invite Kyle to eat with us."

"Thanks but no thanks, Dad." Stephanie shook her head. "That's not exactly the kind of date I had in mind."

"Speaking of which, isn't Kyle coming at seven thirty?" D.J. asked. "You'd better get ready. He's going to be here soon."

Stephanie checked her watch and gasped. She'd been nervous about getting ready too soon. She was worried she might ruin her outfit or something if she changed too early. Now she was in danger of being late!

"Yikes! Thanks, Deej," Stephanie called. She raced upstairs and quickly washed her face and fixed her hair. She put on just a touch of blusher and a small dab of pink lipstick. Back in her room she pulled on her long yellow skirt. It had a pattern of tiny white flowers outlined in black, to go with D.J.'s black

70

sweater. She would finish it off with her white sneakers with the big soles. Now all she needed was her baby tee. She still hadn't found the shirt.

Where is that shirt? she wondered. She searched the room again.

Wait! What's that? she wondered. She spied a flash of white under the stuffed animals on Michelle's bed. She threw the animals aside one by one, tossing them onto her own bed.

"My tee!" she cried. *I knew Michelle had it!*

Stephanie grabbed the T-shirt and lifted it in triumph. It had been under Rosemary the Rhino.

"Uh-oh," Michelle said. She was standing in the doorway.

Stephanie looked up. "Uh-oh what?" she asked.

Michelle stared at Stephanie's bed. It was piled high with stuffed animals.

"You broke rule number seven," Michelle announced. "No stuffed animals on Stephanie's bed."

"I know what rule number seven says," Stephanie told her. "But I was the one who put the animals on my bed. So it doesn't matter."

"That's not what it says on the list," Michelle pointed to the list of rules that Stephanie had tacked up. "So you have to do my chore for me tomorrow night."

"No way, Michelle," Stephanie said. "Not this

time. The reason *your* stuffed animals are on *my* bed is because *my* T-shirt was on *your* bed. And that's against the rules too! So that makes us even."

Michelle shook her head. "The list doesn't say your stuff can't be on my bed."

"It says no borrowing clothes," Stephanie replied. "And you had my T-shirt."

"But I *didn't* borrow it," Michelle argued.

"It's on your bed, Michelle," Stephanie pointed out.

"But I didn't wear it!" Michelle sounded like she was about to cry. "I don't know how it got there."

"Fine!" Stephanie snapped. "I don't have time to argue with you. Just don't cry, okay?"

Those rules were supposed to keep me from getting upset, Stephanie thought. *Maybe I need new rules?*

Just then the doorbell rang.

"We'll finish this conversation tomorrow," Stephanie told Michelle.

"Okay. *After* you set the dinner table for me," Michelle added. "That's my chore tomorrow."

Stephanie ignored Michelle. She threw on the baby tee and D.J.'s sweater. She glanced in the mirror.

The shirt was a little wrinkled. But the lacy sweater covered most of it. And the rest of her outfit looked great, Stephanie thought.

She dashed downstairs. She wanted to be the

first to talk to Kyle. But when she got downstairs, Kyle and her dad were already shaking hands.

"Nice to meet you, Mr. Tanner," Kyle was saying politely.

"Bye, Dad," Stephanie said. She pushed Kyle toward the door.

"Don't you look nice," Danny told Stephanie. He was beaming at her proudly.

Stop that, Stephanie wanted to tell him. *You look like I've never had a date before!*

"Are you sure you two don't need me to pick you up after the movie?" Danny asked.

"That's okay, Mr. Tanner," Kyle said. "My brother's going to pick us up and bring us home. He's waiting out in the car."

Danny peeked out the window.

Oh, please, don't ask to meet Kyle's brother, please! Stephanie prayed. *Kyle will think I'm such a baby!*

Instead Danny said, "What a shiny car. Look how it sparkles."

Stephanie breathed a sigh of relief.

"Polished it myself last weekend," Kyle explained. "It's my brother's car. But I like to help him keep it in its prime."

Danny nodded, impressed. "Did you use a buffer or polish it by hand?"

"Oh, I always do both," Kyle replied. "Once I've

73

used the buffer, I polish with a special cloth. The extra effort pays off. Plus I vacuumed, shampooed the carpets, and treated all the interior vinyl."

Stephanie noticed her dad was beaming. *Great, great, so Kyle's a neat freak too.*

"Okay, okay," she said. "The movie, Kyle? Remember?"

But Kyle was just getting started.

"Then I applied an air freshener and put this special coating on all the tires," Kyle added.

"Have you ever tried steam cleaning the engine?" Danny asked. "I really recommend it—"

Stephanie put her fingers to her mouth and whistled. Kyle and Danny jumped.

"Remember the movie?" Stephanie pointed to her watch. "We don't want to be late!"

Kyle smiled. "See ya, Mr. Tanner," he said.

"Keep up the good work," Danny replied. He wagged a finger at Stephanie. "And don't forget, young lady. Ten o'clock. On the nose."

Stephanie rolled her eyes. "How could I forget? A rule is a rule."

She turned to go. "Wait!" she heard.

Michelle hurried down the stairs. "Are you going to see *The Mermaid's Garden?*" Michelle asked.

"We haven't really decided which movie—" Stephanie started to say. She reached for the front door.

Kyle cut her off. "We're seeing *Cry at Red Dawn*," he said.

"We are?" Stephanie said. *But I already saw that movie*, she thought.

Oh, well. At least she was finally on her date with Kyle. Whether she liked the movie or not.

Stephanie sipped her glass of ice water. She and Kyle had just been seated at China Gardens in the mall. Wo Hop was Stephanie's favorite Chinese restaurant, but China Gardens was pretty good too.

"I'm glad you picked a Chinese restaurant," Stephanie said. "I love Chinese food."

"Really?" Kyle asked. "That's lucky. It's my favorite too."

Kyle smiled at her but was silent again.

He had been pretty quiet ever since they sat down. It made Stephanie sort of uncomfortable. She decided to take Joey's advice. She would tell Kyle a funny story to break the ice.

"When my sister Michelle goes to Chinese restaurants, she has trouble reading the menu," Stephanie began. "One time I ordered wonton soup. Michelle said, 'That's a lot of soup!' She thought I was going to get one *ton* of soup!"

Kyle laughed politely.

"Actually wonton soup is my favorite," Stephanie continued. "That, with moo shu chicken and an ice cold soda, is my favorite Chinese meal."

The waiter appeared to take their order. Stephanie opened her mouth, but Kyle spoke first.

"Sweet-and-sour shrimp and egg-drop soup," Kyle said.

"And for you?" the waiter asked, turning to Stephanie.

"That's for both of us," Kyle answered.

Stephanie stared at Kyle. No one had ordered for her since she was five and didn't know which end of a chopstick to use.

She didn't know what to do.

I just told him what my favorite meal was, she thought. *And I didn't say sweet-and-sour shrimp.*

"Don't worry," Kyle said suddenly, as if he'd read her mind. "I'm paying for the food."

"Oh, you don't have to do that," Stephanie said. "We can split it."

Kyle glanced at her as if she were crazy. "Are you serious?"

Stephanie shrugged. "Sure. At least let me pay half."

"No way." Kyle laughed. He seemed uncomfortable. "I'm the guy. So I should pay for dinner."

Maybe that's why he ordered for me, Stephanie suddenly thought. *Because he's paying. I guess that's the way dates usually go.*

But a little voice inside her head spoke up: *Should I let him order for me? Maybe it's better to pay for myself. Then I'll get to eat what I want. Or should he pay anyway, just because he's the guy?* She shook her head in confusion.

Guess I'll have to ask D.J. to explain the dating rules when I get home, she thought.

The waiter appeared with a pot of hot tea. Kyle took the pot and filled Stephanie's small teacup.

I sure would like a nice cold soda instead, she thought. *And I even told him that's what I like.*

"Oh, I forgot to tell you something," Kyle said. "I really liked your troll shirt the other day."

Stephanie could feel herself blush. She wanted to hide behind her napkin. Why did he have to bring up that dumb shirt?

"Actually, it's my little sister Michelle's shirt," she said. "She's nine."

I can't believe I just admitted that! Stephanie thought. She blushed even harder.

"Renee sure got a good laugh out of it," Stephanie said. "I saw her having lunch with you."

Kyle wrinkled his nose. "Renee's all right. She's nice, but she's a little too loud and pushy sometimes—I mean, for a girl."

"Oh," Stephanie said. She pushed her food around on her plate. Suddenly she wasn't very hungry. In fact, she kind of had a stomachache.

Kyle doesn't like girls who are loud or pushy, she realized. *Does that include asking for what you really want? Like cold soda instead of hot tea?*

She grabbed her tea and gulped a mouthful. "Ow!" she cried. She'd scorched her tongue.

"You okay?" Kyle asked. He quickly poured her a glass of water.

"Sure," Stephanie said. She drank the water. It made her tongue feel better. But now she needed that ice cold soda more than ever.

Will Kyle think I'm pushy if I order it for myself? she worried.

"Um, Kyle," Stephanie asked in a meek voice. "Do you think you could ask the waiter to bring me a soda?"

"Sure! Be glad to." Kyle absolutely beamed at her. He really seemed to like being in charge. "Waiter!" Kyle called. "Over here, please."

Kyle ordered Stephanie a soda—the lemon-flavored kind. She really wanted a cola.

Stephanie groaned to herself and sank deeper into her seat. She had better figure out how to act on this date—and fast. Or else she wasn't going to have one thing the way she liked it the whole night.

CHAPTER
9

◆ ◀ ◆ ◆

Kyle insisted on paying for dinner. Stephanie thanked him, and they crossed the mall to the theater. Stephanie quickly took out her money to pay for their tickets. But Kyle got to the window first. Before she even knew what happened, Kyle had bought a ticket for her and was steering her to the doors.

"Two for cinema three," Kyle said. He handed both movie tickets to the usher. He got back the stubs and put them both in his pocket.

Stephanie swallowed. She had wanted to save that ticket! It was going to be a souvenir of her first date with Kyle. But what could she say now?

Kyle, can I have that ticket stub, please? I want to

keep it forever so I can always remember how the coolest guy in school asked me for a date.

None of this date was going the way Stephanie had imagined.

She followed Kyle into the lobby. The refreshment stand was right ahead of them.

"We still have a few minutes before the movie starts," Stephanie told Kyle. "Let's get a snack."

Kyle frowned. "Well, we don't want to miss the beginning of the movie," he said.

"That's true," Stephanie replied. She was thinking that she'd already seen the movie and the beginning wasn't great anyway. "But we have time to get some popcorn," she told him.

"Okay. Sure." Kyle led her to the snack counter.

"I can't really sit through a movie without popcorn," Stephanie told him. "It's practically a rule of mine."

"Sounds good, then." Kyle nodded. "I'll get it."

"That's okay," Stephanie said. "You paid for the tickets, so how about if I get this? Do you like it with butter?"

"No, I don't," Kyle said.

"Okay." Stephanie waited her turn at the counter. She glanced at a movie poster hanging behind the popcorn machine. It showed a mega-monster from the future. Stephanie giggled. The monster looked kind of like Ms. Trent, their social studies teacher. She turned around, about to call to Kyle to make a joke about it, but she changed her mind.

What if Kyle thought she was being loud or obnoxious if she yelled to him across the lobby? What if he didn't think the poster was as funny as she did? She decided to say nothing.

"Two popcorns, please," Stephanie ordered when her turn came. "One with butter and one without."

Kyle stepped up behind her. "Why are you getting two popcorns?" he asked. "I thought we'd share."

"But I want butter and you don't," Stephanie explained.

Kyle still seemed confused, but he shook his head and shrugged. "Okay," he said.

The girl handed Stephanie two containers of popcorn. Kyle pulled out his wallet.

"Wait," Stephanie said. "I was going to pay for these."

"Sure, but only if we were going to get one container," Kyle said, as if he were explaining something to a small child. "I can't let you pay for yourself *and* pay for me."

"You can't?" Stephanie asked. Now what was Kyle talking about?

Did he mean it was her fault that he had to pay for their food again? Was he mad that she wanted her own popcorn?

Stephanie was more confused than ever. She didn't have time to think about it, though. Kyle was already striding toward the theater. Stephanie hurried to catch up with him.

The theater was only half full. There were lots of seats in the middle, where she liked to sit.

"What about over there?" Stephanie asked. She pointed to two seats halfway down. But when she turned to get Kyle's opinion, he wasn't there. Stephanie saw him already walking down the aisle toward the front of the theater.

He didn't even wait for me, Stephanie thought. She hurried and caught up to him in the first row.

"You like to sit all the way up here?" Stephanie asked.

"Sure. I love sitting in the first row," Kyle said. "It's like you're right inside the movie."

Stephanie didn't know what to say. She hated sitting so close to the front. Everybody on screen looked too big and too fuzzy. It gave her a headache.

Now he'll probably choose two seats on the aisle, too, Stephanie thought. She hated the aisle seats. Everyone was always walking back and forth in front of you, going for snacks and sodas. She liked sitting in the center of the row much better.

Kyle moved out of the way so Stephanie could get to her seat. "Just move in one," Kyle instructed. "I like to sit on the end. Okay? Great," Kyle said.

Stephanie sank into her seat. "Yeah, great," she muttered.

The movie came on. The lead actor's hair was even weirder than she remembered. And the lead actress had on so much makeup you could see it cracking.

Stephanie was dying to make a joke about it. But she didn't want Kyle to think she was pushy. She wished Allie or Darcy were there. They would have laughed their way through the movie.

Finally Stephanie couldn't take it anymore. She had to say something.

She leaned close to Kyle. "Don't you think that guy looks like Mr. Assante?" she whispered. Mr. Assante was a teacher at school, and he was so handsome everyone thought he could have been an actor.

"Shhh," Kyle whispered back. His eyes were fixed on the screen.

Stephanie bit her tongue. She felt her cheeks flame. *Her date just told her to be quiet!*

Stephanie sank down even farther into her seat.

She would have paid attention to the movie. But she'd already seen it, and it hadn't been *that* good the first time. She was completely bored.

For the next few minutes she thought about reorganizing her closet: first the shirts, then the skirts, finally her dresses. She made a list in her head of all the people she had to call. She thought of all the homework she had due Monday morning. She thought of ways to trap Michelle into breaking all ten rules in one day so she wouldn't have to do any chores for years!

Too bad I can't go shopping in the mall and meet Kyle back here when the movie's over, Stephanie thought. He probably wouldn't even notice.

She finished her popcorn and sighed. *Face it,* she told herself. *You're having a terrible time.*

Suddenly the movie was over. The lights came on.

Kyle stretched. "Wasn't that great?"

Stephanie forced herself to smile. "Yeah, great."

She was relieved when Kyle's brother showed up to drive them home. During the whole drive Kyle recapped the entire movie. He kept asking if Stephanie liked this part or that. Stephanie nodded and smiled. She had the feeling that Kyle wasn't listening anyway. He didn't act as if he really wanted to know what she thought.

Finally they reached her house. Kyle walked Stephanie to the door.

"I had a great time," Kyle said.

Stephanie forced herself to smile again. "Yeah, great."

Kyle leaned incredibly close.

Uh-oh, Stephanie thought. *Here it is. The Big Moment.*

Kyle bent down and gave her a kiss on the cheek.

Yesterday she would have melted in her shoes. But tonight, she didn't feel a thing.

Stephanie went inside. She took off her jacket and hung it in the closet. She was heading to the stairs when the kitchen door flew open.

"Oh, hi, honey!" Danny said. "You're home!" He checked his watch. "What do you know, it's ten. Right on the nose. I had no idea."

"You were waiting up for me, weren't you?" Stephanie asked.

"Of course not, Stephanie." Danny smiled.

Just then Jesse and Joey poked their heads out of the kitchen.

"We were just . . . uh," Danny stalled. "Just . . . talking about laying some new linoleum in the downstairs bathroom."

Stephanie heard footsteps racing down the stairs.

"It's ten," D.J. cried. She flew into the living room. "Is she here yet? Oh, Steph! So how was it?"

"Yeah." Jesse grinned. "How was the big date?"

Stephanie sighed. Of course, everyone was waiting to hear about how great her date was. Especially after all the wonderful things she'd said about Kyle.

"How was dinner?" Joey asked.

"Did he hold your hand?" Jesse winked.

"His brother did drive safely, right?" Danny checked.

"Was it fun?" D.J. asked.

Stephanie gulped. What could she tell them that wouldn't be totally embarrassing?

There was a long silence.

"Steph?" Danny said. "What's wrong, honey? Wasn't the date any good?"

"No," Stephanie admitted. "It was a disaster!"

She turned and ran into the kitchen. She flung herself into a chair and buried her head in her hands. She felt as if she would start crying if she even opened her mouth.

The kitchen door swung open. Her father came and sat down beside her.

"Can you tell me about it?" Danny asked.

"I don't even know what happened," Stephanie began. "I've had a crush on Kyle all year. I can't believe that going out with him was so . . . disappointing."

"Was he different from how you thought he'd be?" Danny asked.

Stephanie nodded. "I don't think we have much in common," she admitted. "But it wasn't just that. It was the whole date. I tried really hard. But it just didn't seem to be working."

"Well, Steph, a date shouldn't be work," Danny said. "It should be fun for both people."

"But Kyle wasn't really interested in what I thought about anything," Stephanie said. "Including what I wanted for dinner."

"I'm sorry, honey." Danny sighed. "Dating really is tough. It's hard to know what the other person likes and doesn't like. And people sometimes act very differently when they're with someone they like." He gave her a hug. "Cheer up, sweetheart," he said. "At least you're always yourself."

"Except for tonight," Stephanie said. "That was part of the problem. I wasn't sure *how* to be myself. It was awful."

"Maybe things will seem better in the morning," Danny told her. "I bet Kyle didn't notice half the things that bothered you. And by tomorrow you might decide it actually was better than you thought."

"Maybe," Stephanie said. She stood up and yawned. "I *am* pretty tired. I might as well go to sleep. At least I know that tomorrow can't possibly be as big a disaster as today."

"Bo-ring!" Darcy exclaimed. "Your date sounds like as much fun as . . . as going to the movies with my dad!"

It was Saturday night. Stephanie, Darcy, and Allie were rollerblading at the local rink.

"No, it sounds worse," Allie said. "Because your dad asks your opinion," she explained.

Stephanie shook her head. Her dad had been wrong. Her date with Kyle didn't seem any better today. In fact, it seemed worse every time she told Darcy and Allie something else about it.

"I can't believe it was so bad," Allie said. She patted Stephanie's shoulder.

"I guess the real Kyle is a lot different from the one we imagined," Darcy said.

"I guess," Stephanie said. "But I still have a major crush on him," she added. "At least I *think* I do. But I don't know if I'd go out with him again. That is, if he even wants to go out with me again."

"Maybe he does," Allie said. "Maybe he was just

as nervous as you were, and that's why he was acting that way."

Stephanie hadn't thought of that. She felt a little better. Maybe Kyle *was* nervous and trying to take control of the date was his way of dealing with it.

"Maybe you need to do something with Kyle that you *both* enjoy," Darcy added. She glided a little ahead of Stephanie.

"Yeah. Like rollerblading," Allie agreed.

"Rollerblading?" Stephanie mused. Maybe that was a good idea. Maybe she *should* ask Kyle on a date now. If *she* asked *him* out, would that mean she could decide what they'd do? One thing was for sure—she could plan a better date than Kyle had.

Darcy skated in a circle and glided up to Stephanie on the other side. "Or maybe rollerblading isn't such a good idea," she said in a low voice.

"Why not?" Allie asked. "Steph's great at it and—"

"And Kyle's already going rollerblading," Stephanie finished for her. She stared across the rink.

There were Kyle and Renee. Stephanie couldn't believe her eyes. Not only was Kyle at the rink with Renee, but they were holding hands!

Allie's eyes widened in horror. "Oh, Stephanie!" she cried. "I'm so sorry."

"I don't get it," Stephanie said. "Kyle told me he thought that Renee was too pushy. And too loud. But look at him now!"

"I can't believe he asked her out," Darcy complained.

"Me either," Allie added.

Stephanie tried not to stare. But she couldn't help watching Kyle and Renee. Suddenly Kyle skated to the side of the rink. Renee headed in the other direction.

"She's going to the snack bar," Stephanie said. "Gee, I'm suddenly very thirsty. I think I need a soda."

"I think you have to find out what's going on." Darcy shook her head.

Stephanie followed Renee to the refreshment stand. Renee met Alyssa Norman, one of her fellow Flamingoes. She and Alyssa stood near Stephanie in the long line of people waiting for sodas.

"Kyle is so cute," Alyssa said. "You guys look great together."

"We do, don't we?" Renee laughed. "It's about time we went out. This may turn out to be the best date I've ever had."

Stephanie felt awful. Renee was having a great date!

"I'm so glad I asked him here," Renee added.

Renee asked Kyle! Stephanie's mouth dropped open. It didn't make any sense. Kyle had wanted to make all the decisions on *their* date. Stephanie headed back to Allie and Darcy. She didn't know anything about dating, she decided. But she *did* know that she couldn't stay at the rink one more minute.

The rest of the weekend dragged by. Stephanie couldn't stop thinking about Kyle and Renee. She was so distracted that she kept breaking rules without realizing it. On Sunday morning she had to sort the laundry because she'd been listening to music while Michelle was doing her homework. Sunday afternoon Comet followed her up to the bedroom and Stephanie forgot he wasn't allowed in. Michelle made her clear the dinner dishes for breaking that rule.

Stephanie sighed. She finally had a moment to herself. She needed it to pick out her clothes for the next day. She stared at herself in the mirror.

Not bad, she thought. Stephanie examined the short purple skirt and bright pink tights she was wearing with her tie-dyed T-shirt. She didn't usually wear so many bright colors at once.

She frowned at herself. There was something familiar looking about this outfit. What was it?

Stephanie turned, trying to see how she looked from the back. Suddenly she realized why the outfit seemed so familiar. Renee had worn a bright pink skirt with bright blue tights to the skating rink.

She was dressed like Renee!

Stephanie studied her reflection. It wasn't a bad look, she thought. She picked up her brush and combed her hair with a deep part on one side. It waved over her face, the way Renee's hair did.

"Your hair looks weird," Michelle announced as she came into the room. "What happened to it?"

"Nothing, Michelle," Stephanie said. She brushed her hair back to normal. "Everyone needs a change once in a while, that's all."

"Sometimes people can change too much," Michelle told her.

Uh-oh. That reminded Stephanie of a line in her social studies text. Someone had said that same thing to Amelia Earhart.

My social studies paper, Stephanie thought. She'd completely forgotten about her assignment!

Stephanie had meant to start the essay last week. But first there had been the excitement of getting ready for her big date. Then she had been distracted thinking about how awful the date had been.

And now she had about an hour to come up with something brilliant to say about the changing roles of women and men.

"Okay, Michelle, I've got work to do now," Stephanie warned her sister. "So no more comments about my hair or clothes or anything."

Stephanie pulled out her notebook and a pencil. She sat in her chair and started thinking. But she kept seeing Kyle and Renee. She couldn't concentrate at all. Suddenly she found herself looking at the list of rules she'd written for Michelle.

If only dating were that simple, Stephanie thought. If only there were rules written out somewhere. Then everyone could follow them, and no one would do anything wrong. Or at least they would know when they *had* done something wrong.

That's it! She bolted upright in her chair. *That's what I'll write my paper on!*

Stephanie started writing furiously. She felt happy for the first time in days. She could have a brilliant career—starting with telling guys what girls really wanted.

CHAPTER
10

◆ ◀ ◗ ◆

"What happened to you?" Darcy asked. "There's something different about you...."

It was Monday, and Stephanie had just found Darcy and Allie in the lunchroom. Darcy was staring at Stephanie strangely.

"I don't know what it is," Darcy said. She pressed her finger into her cheek. "But you remind me of someone else today."

Stephanie glanced down at the outfit she'd decided to wear. It was slightly different from the one she'd picked out the night before. It wasn't quite as flashy or trendy.

She had chosen black tights with a black miniskirt, a white T-shirt, a brown suede vest, and matching brown leather boots.

"I thought I'd try something new today," Stephanie admitted. "Although Michelle convinced me not to change my hairstyle."

"Good for Michelle," Darcy said. "I knew that someday you wouldn't mind sharing a room with her."

"One nice comment versus ten thousand annoying ones?" Stephanie asked. "You must be kidding. I'd kick her out in a second if I could."

Especially since I'm the one having a hard time sticking to our rules, Stephanie thought.

"Why, Stephanie! Hello!" Renee Salter appeared beside their table. "Where have the trolls gone? That shirt was so cute, I was hoping you'd wear it again."

"Oh, I'm sure you were, Renee," Stephanie told her. "But if you really like it so much, I'll ask my little sister to let you borrow it. I can bring it in tomorrow if you want."

Renee smiled. "No thanks. I'm sure it looks much better on you."

Stephanie glanced over at her friends. Darcy was studying Renee. Her eyes widened. Renee was wearing pink tights, a pink mini, a white T-shirt, and a black vest. Stephanie knew that Darcy had just figured out who had inspired Stephanie's new style.

"Hey, Steph, hey, Renee!" Kyle stopped next to their table. He balanced a tray full of food.

Stephanie took a deep breath. Was Kyle coming over to talk to her? Or to Renee?

Please, please—don't ask Renee on a date right in front of me, Stephanie silently begged. She couldn't imagine anything worse than being humiliated that way in front of the whole school.

"So, Steph," Kyle began. "I thought we should talk."

Oh, no. It was worse than she thought. Kyle was going to tell Stephanie to her face how terrible their date had been.

"I can explain—" Stephanie started to say.

"—about going out again," Kyle interrupted. "Do you want to?"

Stephanie's jaw dropped. "Want to?" she squeaked. She stared at Kyle's beautiful brown eyes and his wide smile.

Stephanie saw Renee's jaw drop too. She forgot all about their disastrous first date. She had another chance!

"I'll call you," Kyle said. He turned and made his way to a nearby table of ninth graders.

It took a few seconds for Renee to collect herself. She threw Stephanie an angry look and stormed back to her seat.

"Wow." Stephanie sank back into her seat. "Did you hear that? Kyle just asked me out again."

"But why did you say yes?" Allie asked. "Wasn't your date a total disaster?"

"Well, it wasn't great," Stephanie admitted. "But that doesn't mean the second date won't be better. I just can't believe Kyle asked me out in front of the whole school!"

Darcy frowned. "I hope you tell Kyle how you really feel about things this time," she said. "Don't forget how much you hated letting him make all the decisions."

"Huh? Oh, sure, I'll tell him," Stephanie said. She wasn't really paying attention. Why had Kyle asked her out again? Did her different clothes make a difference? Stephanie wondered.

Whatever the reason, Stephanie was thrilled. She had another chance with Kyle!

"I think Greg's essay is great," Carrie Dunbar said. "And another reason it would be good to have female presidents is that we'd have a lot less war."

"Yeah." Ron Martinez snickered. "And we'd all have clean rooms, too!"

All the boys started laughing. Ms. Trent raised her hands for silence.

Stephanie was in her social studies class. They had read five essays out loud so far. And five times someone had made a wisecrack that started an argument in the class.

"Okay, okay. Time for the next student," Ms. Trent said. "Stephanie, would you please read your essay?"

Stephanie glanced down at her paper. She had spent most of the afternoon thinking of ways to make her next date with Kyle perfect.

She cleared her throat and read the title of her essay. " 'The Changing Roles of Boys and Girls: Ten New Rules for Dating,' " she said.

Stephanie hesitated. She wasn't so sure she wanted to read the essay. She had written it when she was angry and disappointed with her date. But Kyle had asked her out again. Now she felt sort of mean, reading her essay to the whole class.

But it was *a bad date, Stephanie*, she reminded herself. *That's why you wrote the new rules. We need new rules.*

True, she argued back. *But if Kyle finds out how I really feel, he might cancel date number two.*

But wasn't she supposed to tell Kyle what she thought? What she liked? What she wanted to do?

Right now Stephanie wished she could forget the whole thing. She definitely didn't feel like reading her assignment to the class. Well, at least Kyle wouldn't find out about it. Eighth-grade social studies assignments were hardly a big topic of gossip around school.

Stephanie continued reading.

"This topic was supposed to be about changing roles in history. Not long ago in this country, women didn't have the right to vote. But now they do. Women have a voice, but the way we live doesn't always let women use it."

Stephanie paused. A low murmur ran around the class.

"Well, another thing that has really changed since women got the vote is the way people date. It used to be that only boys asked girls on dates. That isn't true anymore. Yet people still seem confused about who does what on a date. I decided that we need a new set of rules that will help boys and girls know how to act in this part of the century."

There were a few cheers—and a few boos—from the class.

Ms. Trent clapped. "Settle down, everyone!" She nodded to Stephanie. "This sounds very interesting, Stephanie," she said. "Please continue."

Stephanie cleared her throat. "This is my list," she said.

1. *The telephone has been around almost a hundred years, and everyone knows how to use it. This rule is that girls can call guys.*

2. *Parents always worry about what their kids are doing. So they give them curfews. This new rule is that guys and girls should obey each other's curfews. That way they won't plan a date one of them can't go on.*

3. *Boys and girls may have different interests. They should take turns choosing an activity that each of them likes to do on each date.*

4. *People are moving around the world in greater numbers today than ever before. Which means the selection of foods to eat is also greater than ever. This rule is that guys and girls must agree on what kind of food they'll eat on each date.*

5. *No one is in charge on a date. If a girl wants something, she can ask for it herself.*

6. *The cash register can do amazing things. It can even split a bill into equal parts. Guys don't have to pay for everything. Girls can pay for their own share. Or they can take turns.*

7. *Just because someone pays, it doesn't mean they make all the decisions. Especially if those decisions involve food or drink.*

8. *People used to watch the same movies over and over without being bored. But today there are many movies to choose from. Guys and girls on movie dates*

should make sure they pick a movie neither of them has seen.

9. Before glasses were invented, people didn't have a choice about how they saw things. Some people were nearsighted, and some people were farsighted. Today we can correct our vision problems. So guys and girls can make sure they're sitting where their date is comfortable watching a movie.

10. Computers and telephones help people communicate better every day. And communication is the most important thing to remember about dating. Never make decisions for someone else. Always be willing to compromise.

"These are my ten new rules of dating," Stephanie finished. "It's time for some of the old rules to be thrown out, because the roles boys and girls have now are different than what they were in the past."

Stephanie let out a deep breath. Immediately the room was full of shouting.

"The person who asks for the date *always* pays!" Ricky Forrest called out.

"But why should that person *always* be the guy?" Larry Graves shouted.

"Well, why should a girl do whatever a guy wants—just because he asked her out?" Emily Derring complained. "If he likes her enough to ask her out, why shouldn't she be able to decide what they do?"

Ricky, Larry, and a few other kids jumped up and started shouting out their opinions, but Ms. Trent waved them down.

"That's enough!" she cried, waving her arms frantically. "I never thought this assignment would cause so much discussion," she said. She waited until everyone had settled down. "But now that we've read these short papers, I see this assignment has started some very valuable discussion. This is too important to keep to one class." She glanced around the room.

"I've got a great idea," Ms. Trent continued. "I'm going to ask the principal to let us use the auditorium on Friday afternoon. That way we can debate these issues some more. And I'm going to get my ninth-grade class involved too," Ms. Trent added. "The eighth and ninth graders should debate these topics together."

Stephanie stared at her teacher in shock. What was Ms. Trent saying about the ninth graders?

"I'll pick six topics from all the essays you read in class today," Ms. Trent told them. "I'd like each of you to sign up to speak on one topic. You may speak either for or against each idea. I'll decide on the topics tonight and pass around a sign-up sheet tomorrow."

Everyone started talking at once. Stephanie couldn't say a word. Kyle was in Ms. Trent's ninth-grade class. That meant he'd be at the debate on Friday. Kyle liked doing everything on a date *his* way. If Kyle heard Stephanie's dating rules, they would never go on another date again.

But maybe Ms. Trent won't pick my topic, Stephanie thought. *Then I'll have nothing to worry about. And I'll choose a different topic to speak on.*

This wasn't such a tough problem after all. She could get off easy!

Stephanie gathered her books. She started to leave the class.

"Wait, Stephanie," Ms. Trent called.

Stephanie got a sinking feeling in her stomach.

"Stephanie, that was a very interesting essay," Ms. Trent said. "Dating is certainly a topic close to the minds and hearts of a lot of kids. Thanks for bringing it up. I think it will be great for the big debate."

So much for getting off easy!

CHAPTER
11

◆ ◀ ◆ ◆

"So *now* what am I going to do?" Stephanie complained to Darcy and Allie the next day at lunch. "If I read my essay at the debate, Kyle will know I didn't like anything about our date."

"I thought that was the point," Darcy said. "I thought you were going to tell him how your next date should be different."

"But there might not be any next date if he thinks I don't like him," Stephanie explained.

"But you didn't like him after the date," Allie reminded her.

"I still wouldn't say all this stuff to him straight out. I'd be much more polite about it," Stephanie said.

"You mean like so polite that you don't even bring it up?" Darcy asked.

"That's not fair," Stephanie replied. "I will tell Kyle how I feel. Just as soon as he brings up the date again."

Just then Stephanie saw Kyle and some of his friends walking toward her table on their way out of the lunchroom.

"So what do you think about Trent's big debate?" one of the ninth-grade guys asked Stephanie.

"Uh, it might be okay," she said.

"I think it's kind of cool," Kyle said. "I don't mind expressing my opinion."

I hope that means you won't mind me expressing mine, Stephanie thought.

"And most of the topics are okay," Kyle continued. "Hey, Stephanie, you're in Ms. Trent's class. Which topic are you signing up for?"

"Uh, well . . . I haven't decided yet," Stephanie told him.

Kyle smiled at her. "I signed up for the dating topic. That sounds like a good one. I have a lot to say about the rules in dating these days."

"Really?" Stephanie asked. "That's amazing— because I might choose that topic too!"

Kyle and his friends walked away. Stephanie grabbed Allie and Darcy by the arms.

"Did you hear that!" she almost shrieked. "Kyle picked the dating topic too. At last we agree on something!"

Allie seemed puzzled. "So it looks like Kyle wants to change the dating rules too."

"Guess so," Stephanie said.

"Well, then maybe the debate won't be a big deal after all," Allie said. "I'm glad, Steph."

"Me too," Darcy added.

Stephanie could hardly wait for social studies class that afternoon. She wanted to see the debate sign-up sheet so she'd know for sure that she and Kyle finally felt the same way about something.

As soon as class began Ms. Trent passed around the sheet of paper. By the time Stephanie got it, it was covered with names. She glanced at the various topics.

There was one topic called, "Who Stays Home with the Kids—Men or Women?"

Stephanie remembered that Nora Ryan had argued *for* men staying home with kids. But both boys and girls had signed up to debate against the idea.

Another topic was called "Women at Work— Can They Dress for Success?" Stephanie was surprised to see that Renee had signed up for that topic. Next to her name Renee had written, *I am against women wearing business suits.*

Stephanie chuckled. Renee certainly had an important stand to take about equality in the workplace.

Stephanie quickly scanned down the rest of the sheet. She came to topic six.

Dating, it said. *Should We Change the Rules?*

Stephanie looked at the next line and gasped.

There was Kyle's name, written in neat block letters. And next to his name he had written one word: *No.*

When Stephanie got home, she headed straight for the kitchen. She poured herself a big glass of milk and grabbed a juicy peach. But she was so busy worrying about the big debate on Friday that she hardly even tasted what she was eating.

Kyle *didn't* feel the same way as she did about dating. He had signed up to argue against having any new rules.

What would happen when he heard that Stephanie disagreed with him? Maybe her chances of dating anyone in school would be ruined. What if all the boys disagreed with her? No one would ever ask her out again.

Stephanie really did want to be honest about her feelings. But not if it would ruin her entire social life.

Still, it was wrong to lie about how she felt just to get a date.

She climbed the stairs to her room and fell into her chair with a thud. She threw her feet up on her desk, leaned back, and sighed.

"Uh-oh, Stephanie," Michelle said. She stared at Stephanie from her bed. "I've got some bad news for you."

"Oh, really?" Stephanie asked. "What now? Did Comet accidentally eat Timothy the Turtle?"

"Nope." Michelle shook her head.

"Did Lily the Lion and Mary the Moose have a big fight?"

"Nope," Michelle said. "Uh, you know, they don't really talk to each other. They're stuffed animals."

Stephanie groaned. "I knew that, Michelle. I was joking."

"Well, I'm not joking about this," Michelle said. She glanced over her shoulder at the list of rules Stephanie had put up. "Rule number one, Stephanie." Michelle sighed, as though she were trying to explain something to Stephanie for the hundredth time. "No food in the room."

"So?" Stephanie asked. She looked down and realized she was holding the last of her peach. She popped the whole thing into her mouth and began chewing. "It's gone, Michelle," she said.

"Sorry," Michelle told her. "You'll have to do my chore tonight."

"Oh, come on, Michelle," Stephanie begged. "I didn't mean to bring it up here. I've got a lot on my mind."

"Rules are rules," Michelle replied.

"But I've been doing most of your chores for a week!" Stephanie complained.

"I know," Michelle said. She scooped up an armful of stuffed animals. "That's why I *love* the rules!" She had a fit of giggles.

Stephanie stood up. "Okay." She sighed, giving in. "What's the chore?"

Immediately Michelle stopped laughing and sat up. "Dad wanted me to help him make dinner tonight," Michelle explained. "Something something something casserole."

"Uh-oh," Stephanie moaned. "That's a lot of somethings." The "somethings" in her father's casseroles were always dangerous, Stephanie thought.

That evening her stomach did flip-flops as she watched Danny put his dinner together.

"Thanks for helping me, Stephanie." Danny

smiled as he handed her a spoon. "Stir that, will you?"

"Uh, sure." Stephanie poked at the food.

"So I guess you're doing another of Michelle's chores," Danny said.

"Yeah." Stephanie shrugged. She still didn't want to admit that all the "help" she'd been giving Michelle in the last week had been part of her own punishment. "She was working on something upstairs and I didn't want to disturb her."

"Well, that's just great, honey," Danny replied, beaming at her. "I think your attitude toward her has really changed. It shows you've become a lot more responsible for the family."

Stephanie smiled. *If I were really responsible for this family*, she thought, eyeing the casserole in front of her, *I'd have this dish examined.*

"And I'm going to show you just how proud I am." Danny paused. "I'm going to extend your curfew to ten thirty."

"Really, Dad?" Stephanie managed to say. "That's great."

Except I'll probably never go on a date again, she thought. *So what good is a later curfew?*

"So how's the speech coming, Steph?" Darcy asked over the phone. It was Thursday night. Ms.

Trent's big debate was the next day. Stephanie couldn't believe how quickly the week had flown by.

"I'm still working on it," Stephanie admitted. "But it's not going well. I don't know what to say in front of Kyle."

"Maybe you shouldn't worry about it so much. You two already have another date lined up," Darcy said.

"I don't know if we do," Stephanie admitted. "Whenever I see Kyle in school, he always smiles at me. But he hasn't said a thing about our date since Monday."

"And you haven't called him?" Darcy asked. "I thought that was one of your new dating rules."

"It is," Stephanie agreed. "But I can't call him before the debate. What if he asks me what my speech is about? What will I say? He's signed up to debate *against* new rules."

"He's going to find out how you feel tomorrow anyway, isn't he?" Darcy said.

"I guess so," Stephanie replied.

"Well, Allie and I wish you good luck, Steph," Darcy said. "It sounds like you need it."

An hour later Stephanie was back at her desk. She stared at her "Ten New Rules for Dating" speech. She's been looking at it for so long, she felt cross-eyed.

Her trash can was filled with different versions of her speech. Crumpled paper lay scattered all over the floor. She couldn't figure out what she wanted to say. When she'd written her first essay, she'd been thinking about her bad date with Kyle. Now she was thinking about ruining her second date with Kyle. And it could still be a *good* date.

She already had five notebook pages filled with different lists of rules. But none of them covered everything that Stephanie wanted to say. The trouble was, she still didn't *know* exactly what she wanted to say. All she knew was that what she'd written before wasn't enough.

There was a knock on her door. "Come in," Stephanie called.

The door opened and D.J. popped her head inside. "Hi, Steph," D.J. said.

A second head popped in above D.J.'s. "Hey, Steph, what's up?" It was D.J.'s best friend, Kimmy Gibbler.

"Nothing's up," Stephanie murmured.

"Well, we need some help," D.J. began. "Do you have any old magazines lying around?"

"Only a whole closet full of them," Stephanie

replied. Her closet was stuffed with magazines she was supposed to recycle.

"Can we have them to cut up?" Kimmy asked. She was waving her fingers around like little scissors.

"Yeah, we need to find magazine ads and cut them out. It's for one of my class projects," D.J. explained.

"Sure," Stephanie replied. "But only on one condition."

"If it involves going downstairs to get you food, forget it," D.J. warned.

"Nothing like that," Stephanie explained. "I just need some advice."

"You're *asking* for advice? Okay," D.J. said. She and Kimmy exchanged looks of surprise. D.J. flopped down on Stephanie's bed.

Kimmy hopped onto Michelle's bed. A bunch of stuffed animals fell onto the floor.

"Ooops," Kimmy said. She stared at the animals on the floor.

"Whatever you do, don't put those animals on my bed," Stephanie warned her.

"Why not?" D.J. asked. "Are you suddenly allergic to Lily the Lion?"

"Nope," Stephanie replied. "I'm allergic to doing any more of Michelle's chores."

"What?" D.J. looked confused.

"It's a long story," Stephanie explained.

"That's okay," Kimmy announced. She tossed the last of the stuffed animals back onto Michelle's bed. Then she crossed to Stephanie's side of the room.

"What's the problem, Steph?" D.J. asked.

"The doctor babes are in," Kimmy added. "Spill your guts."

"Well," Stephanie said, wondering where to begin. "It's about Kyle."

"Kyle's the cute guy she went on her date with last week," D.J. explained to Kimmy. "It was a disaster."

"I see." Kimmy nodded. "Then my advice is, forget about him!"

"But I still like him," Stephanie protested. "At least, I think I do. He's one of the cutest boys in school. And he asked me on another date."

"He did?" D.J. asked in surprise. "Why didn't you say anything about it? What are you guys doing this time?"

"Well, I still don't know," Stephanie admitted. "I mean, he asked me out, sort of, but we never really made a date exactly."

D.J. raised her eyebrows. "That does sound like a problem, Steph," she agreed.

"And it doesn't stop there," Stephanie said.

As quickly as she could Stephanie explained about the social studies assignment and the list of rules she'd written.

"So I'm trying to write my speech for the big debate," Stephanie continued. "Only Kyle and I are signed up to debate *against* each other. And Kyle doesn't know it yet." She finished and gazed at D.J. and Kimmy.

"Was my life as complicated as that when I was your age?" D.J. asked. She shook her head in dismay.

"Of course it was," Kimmy said. "But you survived."

"You'll survive too, Steph," D.J. said.

"Thanks," Stephanie said. "But what I need to know is this—should I put my ten rules of dating into my speech? Should I read it in front of Kyle and the whole eighth and ninth grades?"

"Well, what's the worst thing that could happen if you do that?" D.J. asked.

"I'm not sure," Stephanie said. "It's just hard to know what Kyle really wants in a date. He told me he thought this other girl was too loud and pushy, but then he went out with her."

"Not cool," Kimmy said.

Stephanie nodded. "You know, I even wore different clothes to see if that would make a difference to Kyle," she admitted. "I think it did, because that's when he asked me out again. But now I think that wasn't the right thing for me to do."

"It sounds like a bad idea to me," D.J. agreed.

"I know," Stephanie said. "And I think the rules about dating should change too. Nobody should pretend to be different than they really are to get a date. But I'm afraid Kyle doesn't agree. And I'm afraid that if I say how I really feel, Kyle won't want to go out with me again."

"And?" Kimmy asked. She and D.J. exchanged a look.

"What do you mean, 'and'?" Stephanie answered. "He'd never ask me on another date as long as I live."

"And would that really be so bad?" D.J. asked.

"Of course!" Stephanie cried. "He's really popular. And I'd be totally humiliated. Everyone knows we went out the first time. They're all waiting to see what happens next."

"There is another possibility," D.J. suggested. "Maybe if Kyle hears how you really feel, he'll take you on the kind of date you'd really like."

"Huh?" Stephanie said.

"Look, it's okay to want someone to like you,"

D.J. told her. "But they should really like *you*, not someone you're pretending to be."

"So how exactly does this all work?" Stephanie asked.

"Look, Steph," D.J. said. "It's good to decide what's important in a relationship. But one of the first things you might ask yourself is why you want to go on a date with a guy who doesn't think you can order your own dinner."

"That's one of my problems," Stephanie agreed. "I didn't have the best time with Kyle on our date. But whenever I'm around him, all I can remember is how long I've had a crush on him and how cute he is."

"Kyle is very cute," D.J. agreed. "But you were pretty unhappy after your date. Is he really the kind of guy you want as your boyfriend?"

"I don't know," Stephanie said thoughtfully. *Is he even the kind of guy you'd want as a friend?* she asked herself.

"Yeah," Kimmy agreed. "You shouldn't want to go out with him just because other people think he's cute. Or because he's popular."

"I think it's great that you want to make a list of dating rules," D.J. said. "And one of the first ones should be that dating isn't a contest."

"I guess so," Stephanie mumbled.

"It's true," D.J. said. "Whenever you worry too much about what other people are going to think or say, it's always harder to do what's right for yourself."

"But what about this other girl—" Stephanie began.

"Oh, no!" Kimmy interrupted. "Forget about that. There's always another girl."

"I can't forget it," Stephanie said. "It really bothers me that Kyle might go out with her. That might bother me more than whether or not he goes out with me again."

"Is that one of the reasons you don't want to make him mad at you? Because he might ask this other girl on a date?" D.J. asked.

Stephanie thought for a moment. "I guess so," she realized. "I always get upset when I see them together. Even though my date with Kyle was so disappointing."

Both D.J. and Kimmy nodded in understanding. "Maybe you should stop worrying about whether or not to be honest with Kyle," D.J. suggested. "First you need to start being honest with yourself."

"I hadn't thought of it that way," Stephanie confessed.

D.J. stood up. "Were we any help?" she asked.

"Yeah. It's still a lot to figure out," Stephanie admitted. "But you guys really helped."

"Great!" Kimmy cried, sticking out her hand. "Do you want to pay the doctor babes now? Or should we bill you later?"

Stephanie laughed and shook her head. "Later," she said.

"Just remember, kid," Kimmy told her. "Guys are the major crisis in every woman's life."

"Yeah, good luck, Steph," D.J. added. She and Kimmy left the room, clutching stacks of old magazines.

"Thanks," Stephanie mumbled. "I'm going to need it."

Stephanie stared down at her notes.

Her date with Kyle *wasn't* the best date in the world. But Stephanie didn't want it to be the last date she ever had.

She picked up her pen and started writing. She still had one thing to look forward to. No matter what she wrote in her speech, the debate would be over in just one more day.

CHAPTER
12

◆ ◀ ◆ ◆

Last period Friday afternoon finally came. It was almost time for the big debate. Stephanie was a wreck. She had managed to write a speech. But she wasn't sure if it said any of the right things.

"Are you ready, Steph?" Darcy punched her lightly on the shoulder.

"I guess," Stephanie muttered. She tossed her books into her locker and slammed it shut.

"You're just nervous," Darcy said.

"Well, don't be afraid of saying the wrong thing. You know how debates are. Nobody really listens," Allie said.

Stephanie shot her a look.

"Just kidding," Allie said.

Stephanie gave her a weak smile.

"You'll be great," Darcy predicted. "You always are."

"I don't know," Stephanie said. "This time I think I'm just as confused as anyone else."

The bell was about to ring. Swarms of eighth and ninth graders were making their way down the halls to the auditorium.

Stephanie and her friends fell in step with the crowd. They were about to go through the side doors of the auditorium when Stephanie heard someone calling her name. It was Kyle.

He was trying to push his way through the crowd to Stephanie. "We should talk later," he called.

"We should?" Stephanie asked in surprise. She had been wondering if Kyle was avoiding her. He hadn't said anything about their date since Monday.

"After the debate," Kyle added. He disappeared into the auditorium. Stephanie saw him sit with a group of ninth graders in the front row.

I wonder if he wants to tell me that we aren't going out, Stephanie thought. *Or if he wants to remind me that we are.*

Stephanie, Darcy, and Allie found seats together in the middle of the auditorium. It was soon filled with the entire eighth- and ninth-grade classes. Everyone was milling about, whispering and laughing. The teachers were shushing everyone, but no one was listening.

Everyone's acting like this is no big deal, Stephanie thought. *Maybe Allie is right. Maybe they won't even pay attention.*

Stephanie pulled out her speech for about the twelfth time that day.

She quickly read it over. It mostly said the same thing as her essay. She had thrown in a few jokes to keep everything light. But it still said that girls should have an equal say on dates. That boys and girls should arrive at decisions by saying what they each wanted and then making an agreement they both accepted. It even said that everyone should order their own food in restaurants.

"Bo-ring," she muttered.

Darcy gave her a strange look. "What's wrong?" she asked.

Stephanie opened her mouth to answer, but Ms. Trent interrupted.

"Okay, everyone," Ms. Trent said into the microphone. "Settle down. Let's begin the debate. Our first topic is, 'Should Women Work Outside the Home?' "

Stephanie watched as at least ten students climbed onto the stage.

"I think women should stay home with their kids," Andrew Fogel began. Stephanie recognized him as a ninth grader. "They already know how to take care of kids. And they're better at it. Why take the time to teach someone else who won't do as good a job?"

Allie nudged Stephanie. "Are we really going to have to listen to all of them?" she asked.

"This is going to take forever," Darcy agreed.

There was a burst of applause as the first student finished speaking.

"I disagree." Rob Simmons, an eighth-grade boy, got up to speak. "What about single parents? My mother has to work to support us. And she does a great job at it. Besides, not all kids need someone to stay home with them. I take care of my brother and he's—"

"About to go crazy!" someone shouted. There was a burst of laughter from the first row.

"Quiet down!" Ms. Trent glared at the boys in front.

The next speaker was Sandy Whiting, a girl in Stephanie's class. "I think that if women who are single parents can work, then married women should have the same choices. And instead of the wife, why can't the husband stay at home?"

There were murmurs through the audience. The debate was going pretty quickly. Everyone had their own opinion, and they were all eager to take turns speaking. Some kids got up from the audience even though they weren't signed up to debate a topic.

"No way are girls as good at sports as boys. And that's final!" insisted Tim Weston, a ninth-grade basketball player. It was the third time he'd screamed that. The next thing he knew, he was being led out into the hall.

"Thank you," Ms. Trent said into the microphone. "Our next topic is 'The Workplace.' Renee Salter will start us off."

The crowd applauded politely except for a pink row of Flamingoes, who whooped and screamed.

Renee sauntered toward the microphone. She flashed her fellow birds a blinding white smile.

"I think it's criminal that women should have to wear business suits to work," she began. "Why should women have to look like men? Everyone knows women have a much better sense of fashion. Why shouldn't they be allowed to express that?"

"It figures that Renee would find a way to talk about clothes." Darcy snickered, shaking her head.

Stephanie frowned. "It's true that Renee cares about her wardrobe more than anything else," she said. "But I have to admit she kind of has a good point."

"Really?" Darcy seemed surprised.

"I guess she does make *some* sense," Allie said.

"Women spend a lot of money on how they look," Renee finished. "A wardrobe isn't just a bunch of clothes. It's a reflection of your personality."

When Renee was done, Stephanie, Darcy, and Allie joined in the applause.

"This debate is much more interesting than I ever expected," Allie whispered to Stephanie.

Allan Gross, a dweeby guy in the ninth grade, stepped up to the microphone. "Work isn't about showing off your personality," he began. "It's about doing the job."

Arlene McVay, a girl Stephanie knew from the newspaper staff, was next. "If women want respect from men, they have to look serious," she said. Arlene was wearing her usual outfit: a striped button-down shirt and chinos.

Arlene finished speaking.

"Our next top is 'Dating: Should We Change the Rules?'" Ms. Trent announced.

"Here we go, Stephanie," Darcy said excitedly. "Here's your topic!"

"First up, Kyle Sullivan," Ms. Trent announced.

Stephanie watched Kyle stride confidently up to the microphone.

"He's so cute," a ninth-grade girl next to Stephanie whispered.

Yeah, Stephanie agreed.

"Guys should take care of girls," Kyle started off. "Men have always gone out and earned money and brought home the food. It's a guy's role to hold open doors and pull out chairs and stuff like that. Like picking out a movie. It's just protecting a girl so she doesn't have to decide. Why should she be bothered? It's being a knight in shining armor, and everyone knows that's what girls want."

"Not this girl," Stephanie said under her breath.

"It used to be that way," Kyle continued, "and I just think it should change back. It makes things simple. And there aren't any surprises."

Stephanie was sure he was speaking right to her.

"At least he means well." She sighed.

Kyle finished, and Stephanie noticed that most of the guys in the audience applauded loudly. She was feeling more and more uncomfortable. She frowned at her own notes. Something was really bothering her.

She remembered something she'd heard Becky say the other day. She hadn't understood it when Becky said it, but now it made sense: *Sometimes the best rule is that there aren't any rules.*

Suddenly Stephanie realized what had been bothering her about her own essay. She was still thinking about rules—*new* rules versus *old* rules. That's where she was wrong.

"Our next speaker is Stephanie Tanner," Ms. Trent announced.

Stephanie thrust her notes at Darcy. "Here, hold these for me, will you?"

Darcy glanced at Stephanie in surprise. "What are you doing?" she asked.

"Throwing out my speech. What does it look like?" Stephanie replied.

"But how will you know what to say?" Allie asked.

"I'm going to say what I really feel," Stephanie answered. She hurried to the stage.

The audience quieted down as Stephanie cleared her throat. Her heart was pounding, but she was bursting to speak.

"I had a speech all written out," Stephanie confessed. "I was going to come up here and say that there had to be rules to make dating more equal. And more fair than what Kyle was describing. I was going to say that there should be new rules. That girls could pay for themselves and that girls and guys should decide together what movie they're going to see. That they should decide what to do on a date together. That kind of stuff."

Stephanie cleared her throat again.

"But I see now that the real point is to get rid of the rules," she went on. "Especially the ones that don't help. Men and women have fought hard to make sure that people have the freedom to make their own rules, as they need them."

The audience was quiet. Stephanie swallowed the lump in her throat. Everyone was listening to her. Ms. Trent nodded at her in encouragement.

"What's really important is that people be true to themselves," Stephanie went on. "Nobody should change to be the way someone else wants them to be. Nobody should dress a certain way just to get someone else to like them. They shouldn't change what they really believe in. They shouldn't hide their true feelings." She paused and took a deep breath.

"If I had to have a rule, it would be that there would be no rules," Stephanie said. "Just listen to what you really feel and stick to who you are. Thank you."

The auditorium erupted in wild applause. Darcy and Allie were whistling from the audience.

Stephanie saw Kyle sitting quietly in the front row. His arms were folded across his chest. He didn't look happy or sad. He just looked kind of serious.

Stephanie remembered how much fun her date *wasn't.* She felt as if an enormous weight had been lifted off her shoulders. She had finally said what she truly believed! And in front of the entire eighth and ninth grades. It was official!

CHAPTER
13

◆ ◀ ◆ ◆

"Congratulations, Steph!" Darcy squealed. She threw her arms around Stephanie's neck so hard she almost choked her. "You were fantastic!"

"Yeah," Allie agreed, grinning. "Didn't we tell you that you'd know what to say?"

"You sure did," Stephanie said.

They were standing in the hall outside the auditorium. All around them groups of kids stood talking. It seemed as if nobody wanted the debate to end. Stephanie even heard lots of people talking about dating. Ms. Trent was right. It was a topic kids really cared about.

And people kept coming over to congratulate her. "You did a great job," Arlene McVay said.

"Super!" Rob Simmons agreed.

Stephanie was surprised to see Renee edging close to her.

"Uh, that was pretty cool, what you said," Renee muttered.

"Thanks." Stephanie grinned. She felt really good about what she'd said. Even if Kyle *did* ask Renee out now, it wouldn't bother her. Well, not *too* much.

Suddenly she spotted Kyle making his way through the crowd toward her.

"I can't believe it!" Allie whispered.

Darcy nudged Stephanie in the ribs. "I wonder what he's going to say? That you're the smartest person in the school?" she joked.

"That he's turning over a new leaf and wants to let you plan an entire date," Allie guessed.

Stephanie poked both her friends to be quiet. Kyle stood in front of her. He cleared his throat.

"Stephanie, I, uh, was pretty surprised to hear what you said," Kyle began.

"Well, I didn't really get a chance to tell you how I felt before," she admitted. *And I guess this means no second date,* she thought.

Kyle nodded. "I just wanted to say that I think you're right."

Stephanie's jaw dropped. "You do?"

"Yeah," Kyle said. "I'm sorry I decided what to eat and what movie we should see."

Stephanie noticed Renee listening to Kyle.

"I was thinking that maybe we should see that Christian Slater movie you mentioned," Kyle continued. "The early show on Saturday gets out in time for your curfew."

Renee burst out laughing. Stephanie cringed.

"Stephanie? You have a curfew?" Renee said loudly. "I guess you have to get the Troll family to bed—"

A few Flamingoes standing nearby tittered.

"Cut it out, Renee," Kyle said. "I happen to know that you have a curfew too."

Renee blushed and stomped away.

Stephanie smiled. "Thanks for sticking up for me," she told Kyle. "Actually my curfew is extended a half hour."

Kyle grinned. "Great! So I could pick you up at seven thirty tomorrow night."

Kyle looked so cute that Stephanie almost said yes. "Well, Kyle, I don't think that will work," she said instead. "I'm busy tomorrow night."

Kyle's jaw dropped. "What do you mean?"

"I mean, maybe we shouldn't go out again right away."

Stephanie heard Darcy and Allie gasp.

"I don't get it," Kyle said. "Didn't we have a date? You already said you'd go out with me."

"But we never really talked about it," Stephanie tried to explain. "You never actually *asked* me. All you ever said was that we *should* go out again." Stephanie shrugged. "And it is Friday. So I've already made plans for tomorrow."

Kyle frowned. "Well, what if we saw the new Keanu Reeves movie, then? It gets out at ten."

"I don't think so," Stephanie told him.

Kyle scratched his head. "I don't understand. I thought you wanted me to do things your way."

Stephanie shook her head. "You missed the point, Kyle. You're trying to guess what I want. You're *still* not *asking* me. Listen, I'll give you a call if I change my mind, okay?"

Kyle shrugged and turned away. Stephanie watched as Renee followed him down the hall.

"If they end up going out this weekend, it will be your own fault," Darcy pointed out.

"Why did you turn him down?" Allie asked. "Weren't you the one who wanted to make date number two perfect?"

"That was before I realized I didn't want to go on date number two," Stephanie said. "I finally realized that we just don't have that much in common. The point of a date isn't just to be the one making the decisions. It isn't about finding a good way to compromise. It's also about having fun."

"Maybe it would have been different if you acted more like yourself," Allie suggested.

"Yeah, maybe it's not over for you two," Darcy said.

"Maybe not," Stephanie agreed. "After all, I never did get around to asking *him* on a date!"

"You're telling us that Kyle asked you to the movies again and you said no?" D.J. shook her head in wonder. "Wow."

"I know," Stephanie said. She was still amazed at how good she felt about everything.

It was later that afternoon. Stephanie was in the living room with D.J., Danny, Becky, and the twins. She'd just finished telling them all about the big debate at school.

"I guess you won't be using that new curfew of yours right away," Danny said.

"I guess not," Stephanie agreed.

"I still can't believe you turned Kyle down," Becky said. "That was pretty brave."

"I was actually true to myself," Stephanie said. "And I have to thank all of you for your advice. But especially Alex." Stephanie bent down to give her little cousin a kiss on the cheek.

"Alex?" Danny laughed. "What kind of advice did he give you?"

"Oh, just a little lesson in hide-and-go-seek," Stephanie said. She grinned at Becky.

"Becky and I were playing hide-and-seek with Michelle and the twins," Stephanie explained. "Alex got stuck while he was hiding in a closet. He was crying when we finally found him. He was 'out' and he should have been 'it.' But he wanted to hide again."

"I remember," Becky said. "Michelle told Alex he couldn't hide. He had to be 'it.' That's the rule."

Stephanie nodded. "But Alex was so upset that Becky said, Why don't we let him hide again?" Stephanie smiled at Alex. "After all, the real point of the game was to have fun."

"Oh, I see," Danny said. "Alex taught you a lesson in when to bend the rules."

"Or break them," Stephanie agreed. "I remembered it just in time for the debate. I finally realized I was too worried about what Kyle wanted and the right way to do everything. I completely lost sight of the fact that a date is supposed to be fun."

"Now that *is* a great lesson, Stephanie," Danny agreed. "I'm really proud of you."

"So what new rules did you come up with?" Becky asked curiously.

"The rule that says there shouldn't be any rules," Stephanie said. "And to think I owe it all to a game of hide-and-seek!"

"Hideseek!" Alex squealed. He and Nicky dashed away and hid inside a nearby closet.

Everyone laughed. Danny, D.J., and Becky stayed downstairs to play with the twins. Stephanie headed up to her room.

She had to be alone. She lay on her bed and kept playing and replaying the moment when she turned down Kyle's date. Suddenly Michelle burst in without knocking. She took two steps into the room and stopped dead in her tracks.

"Oops," she said. "I just broke the entering-without-knocking rule."

Stephanie laughed and sat up. "It's okay," she said. She hurried across the room and reached for the list of rules on her bulletin board. She ripped it off. Then she tore it into pieces and dropped them into the trash.

"I think this will make us both happy," Stephanie said.

Michelle's eyes widened. Then she clapped. "Thanks!" she cried. "And if you want to make me really happy, you'll take me to see *The Mermaid's Garden* on Saturday."

Stephanie rolled her eyes. "Okay, fine," she said.

Michelle looked shocked. "What did you say?"

"I said okay, fine," Stephanie repeated.

"Really? You'll take me to the movies?"

"Really."

Michelle looked troubled. "But . . . ummm," she said.

"What's wrong now?" Stephanie asked.

"There's one tiny problem," Michelle answered. "It's Dad's rule, the one that says we have to pay for movies out of our allowance." Michelle swallowed hard. "I don't have any more allowance left."

Stephanie laughed "What did you spend it on?"

"Bubble gum," Michelle admitted.

"Don't worry about the money, Michelle," Stephanie told her. "This date is my treat. Because as you just proved, some rules are made to be broken."